SO-AFZ-086

# The Case of the Crooked Kids

*Also by*
**TERRANCE DICKS**

*The Baker Street Irregulars* in
THE CASE OF THE MISSING MASTERPIECE

**The Baker Street Irregulars** in

# THE CASE OF THE CROOKED KIDS

## Terrance Dicks

ELSEVIER/NELSON BOOKS
New York

Library of Congress Cataloging in Publication Data

Dicks, Terrance.
    The Baker Street Irregulars in the case of the
crooked kids.

    Half title: The case of the crooked kids.
    SUMMARY: A group of young English sleuths help the
police uncover a ring of teenage criminals masterminded
by an older gang of crooks.
    [1. Mystery and detective stories] I. Title.
II. Title: The case of the crooked kids.
PZ7.D5627Bai  [Fic]  80–19528
ISBN 0–525–66711–3

Published in the United States by Elsevier/Nelson Books, a division of Elsevier-Dutton Publishing Company, Inc., New York.

Printed in the U.S.A.                          First U.S. Edition

10   9   8   7   6   5   4   3   2   1

# Contents

# The Case of the Crooked Kids

# Prologue

It was a really professional job. To start with, the time was right. Not the traditional dead of night, when burglar alarms are switched on and watchdogs alert. When every little creak gets an anxious householder out of bed, and patrolling policemen are alert for travelers with suspicous-looking bags. This was the middle of the *evening*, supper over, kids wrestling with homework, teenagers out enjoying themselves, and parents slumped in front of the TV, struggling to decide between *Starsky and Hutch* and a BBC documentary about Chinese agriculture.

After midnight the big detached house was like a fortress—but not at this hour. The burglar slipped over the garden fence, climbed up the elm tree that grew near the back of the house, swung across to the drainpipe, and got in through the half-open bathroom window. It was the tiniest of spaces, but it was big enough for him.

Inside the bathroom he stood very still, alert for any sound of movement. This was the third-floor bathroom —there was one on each of the other two floors. No reason for anyone to use this one until bedtime. Still, no sense in taking chances. Satisfied, he slipped out of the bathroom and moved silently along the thickly carpeted corridor toward the main bedroom. Third door on the right, just as they'd told him at the briefing.

The curtains were drawn and the big room was in semidarkness. He had a moment of nervousness, then got a grip on himself and went inside. Like the corridor the room was thickly carpeted and his feet made no sound. A silk-curtained double bed dominated the center of the room, and just to the left of it was a painting—people in old-fashioned clothes standing about in a garden. He tugged the right-hand side of the frame with gloved fingers and it swung open, revealing the metal door beneath.

For a moment he studied the safe, remembering his instructions. From the bag on his shoulder he took a package of gray plasticlike substance, a detonator, a battery, and a length of electric cord. He packed the plastic explosive into the lock, jammed home the detonator and retreated to the other side of the room, playing out the cord. Crouching down behind a corner armchair, he threw the switch. There was a kind of dull thump, and the safe door swung open.

The burglar looked along the row of shelves inside the safe, remembering his instructions. Ignore the papers and the share certificates. Cash and jewelry only. He began emptying the contents of jewelry boxes into the bag, tossing the neatly stacked bundles of notes on top.

A few minutes later he was closing the safe door and swinging the picture back into place. He looked around the room. Everything in place, nothing to send people rushing to the phone to dial 999.

He was hurrying back along the passage toward his escape route when suddenly he stopped. One of the doors was half open, giving a view of a small, brightly decorated room with a single bed. The walls were covered with pop-star posters, the floor littered with toys from a corner cupboard. The burglar paused, his attention riveted. There it was, tossed casually on the bed, the most beautiful thing he'd ever seen.

Despite his instructions, this was too much to resist. Stuffing the model engine into his bag, the burglar hurried back to the bathroom, climbed out of the window onto the drainpipe, jumped across to the tree, and made his getaway.

# 1

## The Hunch

Dan Robinson, his three friends Jeff, Liz, and Mickey, and the huge shapeless dog called Baskerville stood on the sidewalk outside 221B Baker Street—or rather on the spot where 221B would have been, if it weren't for the fact that an enormous office building occupied the site.

They weren't, as you might think, trying to pay a call on Sherlock Holmes. They were having their pictures taken for the newspapers.

The photographer, a trendy-looking young man in purple jeans and a mauve windbreaker, surveyed the little group, trying to sort them out in his mind. The tall, thin, sharp-faced kid was Dan Robinson. The stocky fair-haired boy was his best friend, Jeff Webster. The skinny fair-haired girl was called Liz Spencer, and the little kid with the bristly hair and ears like jug handles was Mickey Denning.

The photographer frowned. "Still not quite right," he muttered. "Needs something else, a touch of color . . ." He rummaged in the back of his station wagon, produced a tattered deerstalker hat and held it out to Dan. "Tell you what you do, sonny, you put this on."

"No, I don't," said Dan.

"You what?" The photographer was baffled. Most people were so keen to get their picture in the papers they did as he said without question. "Now look here . . ."

"No, you look. I don't mind having our pictures taken to illustrate Liz's mother's article. I don't even mind trailing all the way down here to Baker Street because you thought it would be a nice publicity gimmick to take our pictures on Sherlock Holmes's doorstep. But if you think I'm going to make an idiot of myself, or of Sherlock Holmes . . ."

There was such anger in Dan's voice that the photographer took a step back. "All right, son, all right, no deerstalker," he said pacifically. "It's all real to you, isn't it?"

"What is?"

"Sherlock Holmes and all that."

Dan grinned, a little ashamed of his outburst. "It's real to thousands of people. Do you know people still send letters to Sherlock Holmes? Asking him to take on new cases, find missing relatives?"

The photographer arranged and rearranged the little

group, took what seemed like hundreds of shots, then jumped back into his car. He turned to Liz's mother. "That's it, I reckon. Want a lift back to Fleet Street?"

Liz's mother fished a pound note from her bag. "Can you find your own way back?" She produced another pound. "Here, have some ice creams or something." She jumped into the car and it zoomed off.

As they drove away she turned a little anxiously to the photographer. "I'm sorry Dan was a bit rude. He's an odd sort of boy—very independent."

"That's all right," said the photographer amiably. "Kid knows his own mind. Not many people do these days. Imagine people still writing to old Sherlock Holmes, though. I mean everyone knows he's been dead for years!"

Back in Baker Street, Liz said severely, "You do realize that was one of the top Fleet Street photographers?"

"Top photographer I'll bet," said Jeff. "You saw how many shots he took with his flash Leica? Must have been hundreds. Bound to be one or two good ones in all that lot—law of averages!"

Mickey had his eyes fixed on the pound notes in Liz's hands. "What about those ice creams?"

Liz handed Dan one of the pound notes. "There you are. The price of fame!"

They bought their ice creams from a stall in Regent's Park. At Mickey's insistence everyone had a bunny rabbit—an extra large cone with *two* chocolate flakes sticking up like rabbits' ears. In his view, if someone gave you a pound, it was madness to buy less than a pound's worth of ice cream.

As they wandered through the park eating their cones, Dan's mind went back to how it had all begun. Last half-term holiday he and his three friends had decided to have a shot at solving a mystery—-the theft of a valuable painting from their local "stately home." Since Dan was a keen Sherlock Holmes fan, they had christened themselves the Baker Street Irregulars, after the gang of "street Arabs" who assisted Sherlock Holmes in some of his cases. Thanks to some surprisingly accurate deductions by Dan, and a good deal of enterprise by the rest of the group, they had actually succeeded in recovering the painting.

The whole thing had made quite a splash at the time, and even now, some weeks later, there was still enough interest for Liz's mother, who was a free-lance journalist, to be able to sell an article to a newspaper—hence this morning's business with the photographer. Dan hadn't really cared for all the publicity in the first place, and by now the rest of the Irregulars were beginning to get fed up with it—except perhaps for Mickey. Youngest and smallest in a large and boisterous family, Mickey felt he was established as a personality in his own right at last. He would happily have gone on giving interviews indefinitely. He was only disappointed he hadn't managed to get on television.

As if echoing Dan's thoughts, Liz said, "It's time we forgot about this Irregulars business."

Jeff nodded, "Yeah, it's all getting a bit of a pain."

Mickey was horrified. "Give it up? I was just thinking it was time we were looking around for another case to solve."

Dan shook his head. "Can't, can we?"

"Why not?"

"It's still term time. Don't you read books? The mystery always starts neatly at the beginning of the holidays, and the heroes tidy it up by the end."

"That's right," said Jeff solemnly. "We can't go solving mysteries in school time. It might interfere with our homework."

Mickey stared at them in horror, and finally decided they weren't, couldn't be, serious. He finished the last of his ice cream and fed the end of the cone to Baskerville. "What I was thinking, see, we could all give up school and open a detective agency." He looked hopefully at Dan. "We could get an office in Baker Street, if you like!"

It took most of the afternoon to convince Mickey this wasn't really a practical scheme. They spent quite a long time in the park—there was cash left for a boat ride. There was a certain amount of difficulty with Baskerville, who hadn't been in a boat before and didn't like it much. It took all their combined efforts to heave him in and out! They didn't go back till the middle of the evening, and Mickey was still at it when they were walking down the hill on their way home. "All right, so we can't open an agency. But if another case turns up . . ." He looked pleadingly at Dan. "I mean, you wouldn't just ignore it, would you?"

Dan aimed a mock cuff at Mickey's head. "If I see

anyone with a mask, a cloth cap, a striped T-shirt and a bag marked 'Loot' climbing out of a bank window—I'll consider the whole matter very carefully!''

Later, when they were going their separate ways, Dan wondered what he really would do if another mystery turned up on his doorstep. Recovering the stolen painting had been a terrific adventure, but it had also been very frightening, and at times genuinely dangerous. Dan frowned, remembering the night two villains had raided his house, intending to put him out of the way.

They were walking through one of the posher streets in the area now, lined with big detached houses.

Lost in thought, with Baskerville ambling along beside him, Dan only half noticed the boy walking along the tree-lined sidewalk toward him. He glanced up automatically as they came level, tugging Baskerville aside. (Baskerville was a friendly dog, and had a habit of putting his paws on the shoulders of anyone he took a fancy to and licking his face. Not everybody cared for it.) He was particularly fond of children, and sometimes sent little ones flying with sheer affection. . . . However, he seemed to take against this particular boy, and gave a low rumble in his throat.

Seconds later the boy was past them and they went on their way. A car passed them, stopped, and drove on. Dan glanced over his shoulder—the boy was gone. Dan was nearly home before he realized that something was bothering him. It took him a minute or two to realize that it had something to do with the boy.

He let himself in—his parents were out as usual—and climbed to his room at the top of the house, a combined bedroom and study, stretching out in his battered old armchair to think things out.

As a sort of mental exercise, Dan began trying to summon up a picture of the boy. He had been small and thin, about Mickey's size. He'd been wearing jeans, a denim jacket, a T-shirt—the sort of things any local kid might wear, and carrying some kind of shoulder bag. . . . Not his appearance then—his manner. He'd made as if to cross the road to avoid them—then changed his mind and gone past with a jaunty swagger. As they'd edged past each other on the narrow sidewalk he'd glanced quickly into Dan's face for a moment, then looked away. All at once Dan realized what was troubling him . . . it was The Look.

His mind went back to a conversation he'd had with Detective Constable Day, known as Happy to his friends. Day was the youngest and most junior detective in the CID room at the local station, a thin, sharp-faced young man who looked more like a crook than a cop. He had been involved in the missing painting business, and Dan's solving of the case had left Day with a well-deserved share of the credit. They'd become good friends, and Dan often dropped around to Day's cramped little CID office for a chat. It was during one of these conversations that the detective told Dan his theory about The Look.

"I can tell a crook just by the look of him, any good copper can," Day had asserted. "I can walk into a pub, or stroll through a crowd and pick out the villains just like that. The real professionals have got something special about 'em. I call it The Look."

Dan had been skeptical. "What look?"

"Ah, well, that's not so easy to explain." Day thought hard. "You see, a villain lives a different sort of life from the average bloke. He's either just done something illegal, or he's thinking about it. Anyone he sees, even a stranger in the street, he automatically weighs them up, sees if they could be a danger to him."

Dan had nodded, interested. "So they look wary?"

"It's more than that. Most villains think a lot of themselves, think they're putting something over the rest of us. At the same time, they're scared, though they try not to show it . . . so they try to look tough. . . ."

"So . . . tough and wary and scared and defiant, all at the same time?"

Day nodded. "That's pretty close. It's a look that says, 'So what if I have done something, you can't prove it!' And 'Don't you mess about with me or it'll be worse for you!' " He sighed. "Maybe I'm not explaining it too well, but it's real enough."

"It reminds me of some old professor's definition of poetry," said Dan solemnly.

"Oh, yeah? And what's that?"

"He said he couldn't actually say what poetry was, but he knew it when he saw it—just as a terrier knows a rat."

"That's it," said Day eagerly, looking very much like a terrier himself. "There must be something in this literature business after all. 'A terrier and a rat!' " Day grinned. "Want to know how to put an end to the crime wave?"

"Go on, tell me."

"You pass a new law, see. Make having The Look a criminal offense. Then you get me and some other good coppers going around with some nice brawny young wollies."

"What's a wolly?"

"Uniformed policeman," said Day. "Don't you know *anything?* Anyway, soon as we see anyone with The Look, we whip 'em inside."

"I think you might find there was a certain amount of opposition to a law like that," said Dan. "Some people might think it wasn't in accordance with British justice!"

"That's just the trouble, isn't it?" said Day triumphantly. "We know who the villains are, but we can't touch 'em! Now, off you go, my lad, I've got work to do."

Now Dan sat slumped in his armchair, remembering that conversation. He remembered Day's words: "Anyone he sees, even a stranger in the street . . ." That was what was bothering him about the boy. He'd had The Look.

Dan rose and stretched, and went down to make himself some tea. Baskerville padded behind him, waving his tail hopefully. He knew he only got fed twice a day, but he never gave up hope. So much for Day's theory, thought Dan, as he put on the kettle. What could a kid that age have to do with real professional crime?

Detective Constable Day was on the carpet. Well, not actually on the carpet, as his little office didn't run to one. In fact, he was cowering behind his paper-cluttered desk while Detective Sergeant Summers loomed over him. Unlike Day, Summers was a very large man, and he filled the little office like a human thundercloud. He slammed a thick file of papers down on the already cluttered desk. "It is not good enough, Day. It is definitely not good enough!"

"No, Sarge," agreed Day.

Summers thumped the desk, sending up piles of dust. "They decide to do a spot check on the crime statistics, right?"

"Right, Sarge."

"And what does that computer tell us? All over London, the figures are holding steady. They're not going down, but at least they're not going up. All except in one area, one black spot on the bright face of the metropolis. And where is that area, Day?"

"Dunno, Sarge," said Day, though he was beginning to have an idea.

"It is here, Detective Constable Day. Here! In this very district!" The massive fist thumped down again, and more dust flew up. "We, and we alone, have a sudden rapid rise in the burglary rate." Summers leaned over his subordinate. "The Chief Inspector is not pleased, Day. The Inspector is not pleased. And, most important of all, *I* am not pleased." Summers stood up. "There is talk of bringing in outside assistance, and you know what that means. We do not want a lot of Flash Harrys from the Flying Squad tramping about on our manor. *Do we, Day?*"

"No, Sarge."

"Right, then." Summers pointed to the papers. "Here is the breakdown of the statistics as they affect this area, and the file on the relevant cases. You, Day, will drop all other work and concentrate on this list—seventeen unsolved crimes! And unless you come up with something, you'd better get your nice dark-blue uniform out of mothballs." Summers paused at the door. "Tell you what, if you find you're not getting anywhere, you can call in your boy detective!" He thundered out, slamming the door.

Day sat staring at the crime list in silence. Summers was being unfair, no doubt about that, passing the buck, so as to be sure of a scapegoat. Day shrugged philosophically. Who ever said life was fair, anyway? As he went through the file he remembered Summers' parting gibe. For a moment Day half considered taking him up on it. Then he shook his head. This was a string of highly organized professional burglaries. Dan Robinson and his Baker Street Irregulars couldn't cope with anything like that . . . could they?

# 2

# Crime Wave

"Well, of course, it was his own fault really," said the girl in the supermarket. "He was in such a hurry to be off Friday night, he left the takings in the safe, instead of taking them around to the night safe at the bank. Monday morning he comes in all bright and cheerful. 'Just off around the bank, then,' he says. You should have seen his face when he opened the safe. 'It's gone,' he said. 'The money's gone.' Well, we had the police here and everything, but it was too late then, wasn't it? There was crates of Coke missing too, and cans of potato chips . . ."

Still chattering, the girl added up Liz's purchases and then put them into a bag.

As Liz carried her shopping away, she made a note to tell Dan next time she saw him. Not that a common or garden-variety supermarket robbery will interest the great detective, she thought . . .

Jeff's dad began unpacking the cardboard box with loving care, arranging his purchases on the shelves of his garage workshop. "They're in a heck of a state down at the hardware shop," he said. "Here, stick that spackle up on the shelf, son."

Jeff took the box and put it on the shelf. "Why, what happened?"

"Just had a robbery. Sid was telling me all about it." Sid was the manager of the hardware shop. He and Jeff's dad were good friends. Not surprisingly, since, as Jeff's mother often said, his dad kept the place going practically single-handed.

"When?" asked Jeff.

"What? Oh, last weekend, apparently. Saturday's his busy day, see, and he takes the cash home so he can bank it Monday morning. Come Monday he opens his safe and there it was—gone!"

Jeff's dad began sorting out the wood sections for the new kitchen cabinet. Not that there was anything wrong with the old one. "Now, then, always remember, the secret of success is to measure the job up properly before you start . . ."

Mickey's father stowed the bottles of light ale in the cabinet under the sink. "They've got this perishing great dog down at the grocery store," he said indignantly. "Nearly had me when I went in. I may have to stop going in there."

"That'll be the day," said Mickey's mum.

Mickey was reading his *AD 2000* comic in a corner, hoping no one would notice him and send him up to bed.

"What did they get the dog for, Dad?"

"Had this robbery, didn't they? Just the other day. Safe blown, money gone . . ."

Mickey's detective instinct was aroused. "Anything else taken?"

"Don't think so—apart from some sweets. Funny, really."

"What is?"

"Well, beer and cigarettes are what they usually go for first in those jobs. They can always find a good home for a crate of beer or a few cartons of cigarettes, no questions asked."

Mickey went back to his comic—but the damage had been done. He had drawn attention to himself.

Mr. Denning looked at the kitchen clock and frowned. "Shouldn't that boy be in bed by now?"

"Just finishing my comic," said Mickey automatically, playing for time.

Mr. Denning reached out an enormous hand, scooped Mickey off the sofa and deposited him on the stairs. "Off!" he said firmly.

As he climbed the stairs to his bedroom, Mickey was thinking about the robbery. It didn't really sound like much of a crime. Still, perhaps he'd drop around and tell old Robbo all the same . . .

When Jeff rang Dan's doorbell on Sunday morning it was Mickey who opened the door, a jelly doughnut in his hand. "Come on in," he said hospitably. "Liz is already here."

Jeff followed him down the passage and into the kitchen. "What's up, somebody call a meeting?"

"It seems to have called itself," said Dan. "Have a doughnut."

Liz passed Jeff a doughnut and sat down. Dan poured him a glass of homemade lemonade. "Now then, don't tell me why you've come. Let me deduce it." He studied Jeff narrowly. "You have come to inform me of some local crime!" Jeff's mouth opened in astonishment, and Dan went on. "At first you wondered if it was worth telling me about, but then you decided you might as well."

Jeff sighed. Once again he'd been trapped into the role of Doctor Watson, perpetually amazed by the brilliance of the great detective. "All right, let's have it. Don't tell me you deduced all that from a few smears of mud on my coat sleeve."

"I deduced it from the fact that Mickey and Liz came around for exactly the same reason!"

They all compared notes about their respective robberies.

"So what does it all mean?" asked Jeff.

"Doesn't mean anything, it's just statistics."

"What do you mean?" said Liz indignantly. "Those were real crimes. Try telling those people in the supermarket they were just statistics."

"Listen, statistics are based on real events. And if the particular trend is strong enough, sooner or later you start noticing it in real life. Everyone knows the crime rate in London is rising all the time. All of a sudden we're noticing that those figures really mean something. People around us are getting burgled."

Mickey felt this was a bit high-flown. "Never mind all that. Are we going to catch the burglars?"

"My dear Mickey," said Dan solemnly. "We are dealing here not with a master criminal, but a socioeconomic phenomenon. Even Sherlock Holmes couldn't do anything about that!"

Jeff wasn't convinced. "You're probably right in a general way, Dan. But so many robberies, in so short a time—"

Liz nodded. "And in so small an area."

"Statistics," said Dan airily. "Just statistics . . ."

But for once Dan was wrong.

Later that evening Dan was in his room, trying hard to concentrate on the history of England in the late nineteenth century—it seemed to consist mainly of a lot of Factory Acts. But he found his thoughts kept turning to crime. Had he been too hasty in explaining away all those burglaries? . . .

He heard his parents come in, and after a moment his father's indignant voice came floating up the stairs. "They just walked in and took the money, I tell you, while they were having a late dinner. . . . Blew up the safe and they never heard a thing."

Dan shot out of the room and clattered down the stairs to the living room below. His father was stretched out in his armchair, wearing his usual expression of mild indignation, talking to, or rather at, Dan's mother, who was stretched out on the sofa.

"Hi," said Dan hurriedly. "Listen, what was that you were saying about a burglary?"

"One of your father's clients had a burglary yesterday, dear," said his mother. "Lives quite near to us, as a matter of fact. Maybe it's just as well we got that ridiculous dog of yours."

"The only person that dog ever goes for is me," said Dan's father. "If we ever have burglars, it'll lick their hands and ask to be taken for a walk."

Baskerville gave a reproving *woof* from the doorway. He wasn't allowed in the living room because he tended to brush against things and knock them over and he'd demolished several vases with exuberant sweeps of his tail.

"Tell me about this robbery."

His father looked suspiciously at him. "Why? There's not going to be any more of this detective nonsense, is there?" Actually he was quite proud of Dan's success as a detective. He just didn't want to show it.

Eventually Dan got the story out of him. Dan's father was an architect with his own little business, and one of his best clients happened quite by chance to live fairly close, in one of the big houses on top of the hill. Discovering they were more or less neighbors, he'd invited Dan's father and mother to dinner. The client was a wealthy antique dealer who sometimes kept large quantities of cash in his house, and last night he'd been burgled.

"There were share certificates and bearer bonds in the safe, but they didn't touch them. Just cash and jewelry."

"And the engine," said Dan's mother.

"What engine?"

Dan's father said, "Apparently Alec had just bought his son a brand-new Hornby engine. The boy had been wanting it for ages. It disappeared the night of the robbery. The kid swears the robbers must have taken it. Alec reckons he's lost it somewhere and was using the robbery as an excuse. I mean, these blokes were obviously professionals. What would they want with a toy engine?"

The man who liked to call himself Fagin looked at the circle of attentive faces. "Now remember—the money, and just the money. Nothing else. Isn't that right, Ratty? No more little slipups like this!" He waved the model engine in his hand.

The boy they called Ratty jumped, and then nodded virtuously.

"You'll see plenty of stuff you'd *like* to have," went on Fagin. "Watches, cameras, hi-fi. But remember, property can be traced, recognized. You've got to use a fence, and that's another risk. Banknotes, that's all we want, banknotes and jewelry . . ." He paused impressively. "That's our first rule, and heaven help the one who breaks it. When he gets out of the hospital he can go back to pinching sweets from Woolworth's." He waved the engine again. "I won't overlook anything like this another time. Clear?"

Everybody nodded, Ratty hardest of all.

"Right, then, gather around and pay attention." He waved toward a pile of equipment on a workbench. "Now, our old friend Bill here will demonstrate how to tackle a simple burglar alarm. There'll be questions afterward, so pay attention. Ready, Bill?"

A massive figure slouched forward from the shadows. . . .

# 3

# Crime School

Detective Constable Day shot up from behind his desk like a jack-in-the-box. "*What* did you say?"

"I only asked if there's been a big increase in local burglaries recently," repeated Dan mildly.

Day grabbed him by the arm. "Now see here, young Robinson, you may be the greatest detective since old Sherlock himself, but when it comes to having information from confidential police files . . ."

Gently Dan freed his arm. "Look, it's not exactly a secret, you know."

"Well, it's supposed to be," said Day gloomily. "How'd you find out? More of your brilliant deductions?"

"Oh, sure. I deduced it from the fact that practically

31

everyone I know seems to know someone else who's been burgled. What's going on?"

"I only wish I knew—" Suddenly Day's voice changed. "I've told you before, Robinson, you may have had one lucky success, but that doesn't mean you can hang around here bothering me all day. Now buzz off." Dan looked around. A burly, hard-faced figure was walking down the corridor past the open door. Without moving his lips, Day muttered, "See you in the market café in half an hour," and bustled Dan out.

A few minutes later Dan was walking thoughtfully down the busy High Street toward the market. Something was going on and the police were worried. Perhaps it wasn't just statistics after all.

The market at the bottom of the hill was a mixture of old-fashioned fruit and vegetable stalls and trendy antique, leather-goods, and denim-clothes vendors. Hippies and hawkers seemed to mix together fairly well, and the café sold wine, cheese, and health food as well as strong tea and bacon and eggs.

Dan wandered around the market for half an hour, then made his way to the café. He met Day on the doorstep, and soon they were sitting down over tea and a sausage roll for Day and a Coke for Dan.

"Sorry about the brush-off," said Day apologetically. "That was Detective Sergeant Summers in the corridor, and you'd just touched on a very sensitive subject."

"I'll forgive you—if you tell me what's been going on." Day hesitated and Dan said, "Come on, you can talk here. That sausage roll isn't bugged."

Day took a bite out of it and studied it suspiciously. "Well, since you seem to know most of it anyway . . ." He told Dan about his recent interview with Summers and the sudden astonishing rise in local crime.

"Any link between the robberies?"

"Only what you might call the professional touch. Nice clean entry, no one ever seen, coming or going. Nothing taken but cash and occasionally jewelry."

"That's not what I heard. They took sweets at the grocery store, Coke and potato chips at the supermarket, and a toy engine at the big house on the hill."

Day looked surprised. "You do have your sources, don't you? I don't remember any of that in the reports."

"I don't suppose it was in the reports. With hundreds of quid missing, people probably didn't bother to tell you."

Day shrugged. "Maybe not. So the thieves got hungry on the job? What does that prove?"

"Don't forget the toy engine," reminded Dan. "Just think about it. Sweets, Coke, potato chips, and toys . . . what does that suggest to you?"

"Kids!" breathed Day. Then he shook his head. "No, it couldn't be. Doesn't fit the pattern."

"What pattern?"

"Juvenile crime. With kids you get vandalism, shoplifting, some crude breaking and entering, and taking and driving away—stealing cars for a joy ride."

"Maybe someone's breaking the pattern . . ."

"It *couldn't* be kids . . . not these jobs. Burglar alarms fixed, safes blown with plastic explosives. They even used a blowtorch on one job . . ."

Dan said, "Look, you know my three friends Liz, Mickey, and Jeff?"

"Your Baker Street Irregulars? What about 'em?"

"Liz's shorthand and typing is better than her mother's—and she can drive a car. Mickey works in his Dad's greengrocer's. He can add up a long and complicated order quicker than any cash register. Jeff's woodwork and metalwork is first class and he's an expert photographer."

Day cocked his head on one side. "Bright kids. What about you?"

"Well, I hate to boast—but I helped to clear up a robbery that had you lot foxed!"

"So what are you saying?"

"I'm saying don't underestimate kids. Unless it's a matter of brute strength, a bright kid can do anything an adult can do."

Day shook his head. "It *couldn't* be kids," he repeated. "Whoever these people are, they're professionals."

"Maybe they are. But what gives you the professional touch?"

Day shrugged, "Experience, I suppose."

"What comes before the experience? What happens when you start as a copper?"

"Well, first of all you go to training school—" Day broke off, staring at Dan.

"That's right," said Dan. *"Training!"*

The respectable-looking old man in the dark suit looked around at his audience. His voice was a little husky, as if he weren't quite used to his role. "Now then, who can tell me what makes a good pickpocket—or dip, as we say in the trade?"

"Light fingers?" suggested someone. There was a ripple of laughter.

The respectable-looking man quelled it with a frown. "That comes last of all. The first thing is—good appearance. Always be clean, tidy, respectably dressed. Look like a scruff and you'll be treated like a scruff. Some of you could do with a bath and haircut!"

This time there was a groan.

The man continued, "But the most important thing of all is cooperation. Your first-class dip *never* works solo. He is one of a team."

Gaining confidence, the old man went on, "This team has three members—the bustler, the whizzer, and the runner." He paused. His audience was hushed and attentive. "This is how it works. The bustler bumps into the mark, distracts his attention. While he's apologizing, the whizzer, or dip, is lifting the actual wallet. *But he doesn't keep it.* He passes it immediately to the runner, who disappears. Now, nine times out of ten you get a smooth job. The team meet up later, divvy up the cash, and dump the wallet. The mark doesn't even notice anything till they're well away. But—suppose something goes wrong? Nine times out of ten, the mark will grab the bustler—who hasn't so much as touched the wallet. He can make all the fuss in the world, let himself be searched. Nothing! An exceptionally keen mark might grab the whizzer—but he isn't carrying anything either! The one man they mustn't get is the runner. If there's trouble, it's up to the first two to crowd around the mark and make a fuss so the runner can get clear. Always protect the runner—that's the first rule of a good team."

There was a murmur of applause.

Gratified, the man went on with his lecture. "Now we come to the technique of the actual dip." He pushed back his sleeves. "The hand, as you will see, is held completely flat, the middle fingers used rather like scissor blades . . . now, let's have a practical demonstration." He pointed. "You be the bustler, you be the runner, you're the dip. And for once, I shall be the mark!"

They began to practice.

"A crime school for kids!" Day was still skeptical as they walked back up the hill. "No, it doesn't fit the pattern, I tell you."

Dan could understand Day's reaction. Most crimes do fall into a pattern of some kind, and it's one of the great strengths of the police that any crime they deal with is very much like a string of other crimes in the past. They've literally heard it all before.

But this very experience can be a weakness when something new comes along. "As I said, maybe someone's breaking the pattern," said Dan.

Day shook his head. "Tell you what it is—some mob has worked out a fresh technique—saturation robbery. Move in on one area, clean it out, then go on somewhere else. They'll finish here soon and start up somewhere else."

"Why start here in the first place?" argued Dan. "All right, this part of London's got its rich sections, but it's got its seedy areas too. A lot of these robberies were small stuff, shops and pubs, hardly worth the attention of the big-time criminal."

They were near the police station by now. "Sorry," said Day. "I still can't see it. But if you are right—it's more a job for you than for me."

"What do you mean?"

Day grinned. "Well—what do you need for kid robbers? Kiddy cops! See you." He disappeared inside the police station.

Dan turned to go home. "Kiddy cops, indeed!" he thought indignantly. Then he smiled. Perhaps Day was right. Perhaps this was a job for the Irregulars after all.

# 4

# The Trap

The conference was held that evening, in Dan's room at the top of the house. Refreshments of lemonade and sandwiches were served, and as usual disappeared pretty quickly. Dan called the meeting to order and outlined the problem of the mystery crime wave.

"I don't get it," objected Jeff. "Yesterday we came to you about this and you convinced us it was all statistics."

"Even I can be wrong—occasionally," said Dan. "Besides, this is even bigger than we thought!" He told them about his chat with Detective Constable Day. "He said it was a job for us!"

"Right, we'll get 'em!" said Mickey confidently. "Imagine the cops coming to us for help!"

"I don't think that's *quite* what he meant . . ."

"He said it was a job for us, didn't he? Then let's get on with it."

Liz looked at Dan. "Where do we start? I mean, this is a whole string of crimes, not just one, like last time. We've got no idea who could be behind it all."

"Well," said Dan thoughtfully. "Apart from the fact that the crimes are being organized by someone with a strong local connection, and are being committed by kids with help and advice from older criminals—I suppose you're right."

"And how do you know all that?" demanded Jeff.

Dan began ticking off points on his fingers. "Local connection, because it's a localized crime wave, centered around this district. Expert knowledge about where the money is, in which safes, in which shops and houses."

"Anybody could work that out," objected Jeff.

"But why do it here? This isn't the richest part of London by a long way."

"How do you know it's kids?" asked Mickey. As usual, he managed to give the impression that he already knew the answer and just wanted Dan to explain it to the others.

"Sweets and toys," said Dan cryptically, and explained about the extra things that had been taken at the robberies. "You can't tell me a professional crook is going to pass up a case of beer and settle for a couple of packs of chewing gum, or a bar of chocolate."

"Anyone can get hungry," said Liz.

"Yes, but what about the toy engine? Unless we can find a master criminal who's mad on model trains . . ."

"All right," said Jeff. "So it's kids. Why can't they be doing it by themselves?"

"Technique," said Dan. "According to Day, all the robberies were really professional jobs. Skillful entry, safes professionally cracked, nothing taken but cash and jewels. . . . It takes experience to work as smoothly as that. Kids don't have experience—but they can learn . . ."

"It all seems a bit thin to me . . ."

"Well, of course it's thin! Criminals don't leave nice big obvious clues, or signed confessions. But name an explanation that fits the known facts as well."

Jeff couldn't.

"I don't see all this helps very much," said Liz. "Even if you're right, Dan, it could still be anybody."

"You're forgetting something. This time we're dealing with a *series* of crimes. In other words, there'll almost certainly be more. That gives us our chance."

"A stakeout!" said Mickey excitedly. He was a great watcher of TV police shows. "That's what Kojak does. They find out where the crooks are going to strike next and lie in wait for them."

"Kojak's got the New York police force working for him," Liz pointed out. "We're a bit more limited. How do we know where to lie in wait?"

"That's the problem! We could work out a list of likely places and set up some kind of schedule."

"Oh, no," said Jeff firmly. "I'm not spending every night for the next six months lurking by someone's safe."

"We need bait," said Mickey. "Like in tiger hunting, where they tie a kid to a tree to lure the tiger."

Jeff gave him a friendly shove. "All right, then, Mickey, we'll try that. You can be the kid!"

"Not a kid kid, a goat kid!"

Suddenly Liz said, "I've got it. We'll use a sibling!"

Even Dan was baffled. "A what?"

"It's a kind of word-of-mouth advertising campaign. What you do is you hire a lot of out-of-work actors and actresses and get them to go around a certain area spreading some rumor. You know, just casually in pubs and shops and cafés. 'Have you heard of this marvelous new soap powder so and so's have brought out? I tried it and it made my washing practically *luminous*. It's so good they're going to put the price up soon.' "

Dan was intrigued. "Does it work?"

"Apparently, sends 'em rushing to the shops. People will believe something they hear casually from a stranger more than they will something in the papers or on television."

"I don't see why anyone would *want* luminous underwear," said Mickey, but everyone ignored him.

"We can't afford to hire a lot of people," objected Jeff.

"We don't need to," said Liz impatiently. "We do it ourselves."

"And how many people can *we* tell?"

"More than you'd think," said Dan. "Each of us must know over a hundred kids at school, at least to talk to. Say we each tell a hundred and twenty-five kids—that makes five hundred. They all tell their parents—that makes a thousand adults. Their parents all tell two other people—that makes two thousand. Those two thousand

tell two people each, so that makes four thousand. They
all tell another two—"

"All right, all right," said Jeff hurriedly. "If you go on
like that, the entire population of Great Britain will
know."

"Know what?" asked Mickey.

"He's got a point," said Liz. "Exactly what story are
we going to spread around?"

Dan had already worked this out. "That there's a large
sum in cash, left more or less unguarded, in *one*
particular spot."

"And where's all this money supposed to be?"

Dan smiled. "I've thought of the very place."

Mr. Denning took a long swig at his pint and put the
glass down on the bar. "I reckon it's scandalous," he
said. "Leaving all that money in the school, especially
with all these robberies. Some people ask for trouble."

His friend looked up from the sports page of the
evening paper. "What money?"

"The Bequest," said Mr. Denning in surprise. "Haven't
you heard about it? Some old geezer who was at the
school years ago just died and left them a lot of money,
all in cash. Didn't trust banks or something."

"Is that right?" said his friend absently.

"So he made these special provisions in the will. The
money has to be delivered in cash, kept on the school
premises, and spent in cash for the good of the school."

"That right?"

"So there it'll be in the Headmaster's office locked up
in some rickety old safe you could open with a can

opener. They've got to keep it in the school at least one night, because of the will, going through the motions, like. . . . But will the money still be there in the morning, eh?"

"Ah," said Mr. Denning's friend. "What do you think of Angel's Delight in the fourth race?"

"Well, I must say it all sounds very careless," said Dan's mother. "Crime is enough of a social problem as it is, without putting added temptation in people's way. Who did you say told you about it?"

"I'm not sure," said Dan. "The story's been all over the school for days."

"Well, I'll bring it up at the next parents' meeting. Still, it's nice about the money. Now they'll be able to get that new slide projector without yet another jumble sale . . ."

"Mystery Cash Bequest for School," said Liz's mother. "Sounds like a good story."

"Oh, you mustn't write about it," said Liz hastily.

"Why not?"

"It's one of the conditions of the will. Any publicity and they lose the money."

Liz's mother shrugged. "There seems to be plenty of publicity already. Everyone's talking about it."

And so they were. Children told other children, they all told their parents, and parents told their friends. The story got back to the Headmaster, who issued an official denial. That made everybody feel sure it must be true.

Details changed in the telling, but the main element stayed the same. A large sum in cash was going to arrive in the school tomorrow, and it would stay in the Headmaster's office for just one night. It was an intriguing piece of gossip, and all kinds of people heard it and passed it on.

Eventually it reached the ears of the man known as Fagin.

It was dark in the school.

Crouched in the corner of the corridor outside the Headmaster's study, hiding behind a stack of paper-filled boxes, Dan thought how sinister the place seemed after hours. The familiar classrooms and corridors were shadowed and gloomy. It was easy to imagine the giant figure of Frankenstein's monster stretched on a bench in the science labs stirring beneath its covering sheet, sitting jerkily upright. . . . You could imagine it lumbering out of the laboratory and lurching toward you. . . .

Dan jumped as a bony elbow jabbed him in the ribs and Mickey's voice hissed, "Someone's coming!" Heavy footsteps were coming down the corridor toward them, thump, thump, thump. . . . The thing was casting a huge shadow before it. Dan half expected to see a giant square-headed figure with a bolt through its neck come staggering around the corner. . . .

The figure that did appear was very different—short, tubby and bald-headed, with a straggling mustache. It was old Pop Daniels, the school caretaker, who was both shortsighted and bad-tempered. Dan and Mickey crouched down behind the boxes as Pop stumped along the corridor and disappeared around the corner.

"What do you bet that's it for the night?" whispered Dan.

Mickey nodded. "Serve them right if all the money does get pinched," he said indignantly. Mickey had told the story so many times he believed it himself.

They had been waiting for a couple of hours, and apart from the scare with old Pop nothing much had happened. Liz and Jeff were out in the playground, keeping watch on the window of the study. Dan reckoned it was less likely that the thief would come that way—if he came at all, that was—since the window was visible from the street, but they had to cover it. As Mickey said, "We'd look a right bunch of nits, hiding outside the door while the thief came through the window!"

They'd taken up their vigil straight after school, using the simple method of staying behind and hiding. Mickey had wanted to come back in the middle of the night, but Dan pointed out that a lot of the robberies had taken place in the early evening, and they'd never get away with staying out all night anyway. As it was, each of their parents thought they were spending the evening at Dan's house.

Meanwhile Liz and Jeff were hiding behind the climbing tree in the school playground. Jeff was pretty disgruntled, since he too reckoned it was unlikely the thief would try this way. The school was a rambling old building with plenty of doors and windows. It was pretty certain that any thief would get in somewhere else and approach the study from the inside.

Or so they thought. Suddenly Liz grabbed Jeff's arm. "Look!" For a second the street that ran alongside the school was empty—and at just that moment a figure slipped over the school gates and disappeared into a shadowy corner of the playground. The shape was so thin and dark and it moved so quickly that it looked almost like a shadow itself, and for a moment they lost sight of it. Then it appeared again, scuttling along the wall toward the window of the Headmaster's study.

Jeff and Liz watched in fascination. There was an almost animallike quality about the intruder's movements, the quick scurry and freeze that you usually see only in mice and squirrels.

The dark shape climbed up to the broad stone windowsill and froze again. After a moment they saw its hands moving busily, presumably forcing the catch, then it opened the window a little at the bottom and slipped through the gap.

Jeff and Liz looked at each other in astonishment.

They'd never really expected to see a burglar, and they had no real idea of what to do now that they had. They began creeping closer to the window. . . .

Dan fished for a sandwich from his knapsack. Perhaps the plan wasn't going to work after all. He saw Mickey holding out a hand in silent appeal. He'd eaten all his provisions in the first few minutes. Dan grinned and passed him a cheese sandwich.

Dan yawned, and his head began to nod. He shook it

to wake himself up, stared hard at the study door—and saw a brief flash of light from beneath it. He nudged Mickey. "There's someone in there!"

Mickey nearly choked on his cheese sandwich. "There can't be. We didn't hear anything."

"Maybe we didn't. But there's someone in the study, using a flashlight."

"What do we do?"

"We find out who it is."

Dan moved quietly to the study door and flung it open.

# 5

# The Burglar

Dan saw a dark figure crouching by the Headmaster's desk, shining a light around the room. It whirled and sprang for the open window—and cannoned into Jeff, who was climbing in from the outside. The figure turned, dodged around Dan, ran for the study door—and tripped over Mickey, who was running in after Dan.

Dan hurled himself onto the prone figure and Jeff jumped on top of him. By the time Liz came through the window there was a struggling heap of bodies in the middle of the floor. Deciding there was no point in adding another to the pile, Liz walked calmly over to the door and switched on the light.

The heap of bodies thrashed around a little longer, and then resolved itself into Dan and Jeff holding down a third boy. Mickey, who'd been on the bottom of the pile, had wriggled free and stood gasping for breath. Now that the light was on, they could all get a good look at their captive. He didn't look very fearsome. He was thin and dark, with close-cropped hair, and he wore black jeans, black sneakers, a black sweater, and a black imitation-leather windbreaker. It was difficult to tell his age. The thin scrawny body wasn't much bigger than Mickey, but the narrow, suspicious face with the watchful eyes seemed to belong to someone older than any of them.

Dan and Jeff got up, heaving their prisoner to his feet.

"Well, now," said Dan. "What's all this about?"

The answer was a string of four-letter words. Jeff, who had old-fashioned views about swearing in front of ladies, gave their prisoner a shake. "Oy, pack that up, or you'll get a thick ear. What are you doing here?"

The prisoner said nothing.

"You wouldn't have heard a rumor about there being a lot of money in the school?" asked Dan.

Still the prisoner didn't speak.

"Search him, Mickey," ordered Dan.

The lad began struggling wildly, but Dan and Jeff held him fast. Mickey went quickly through his pockets, and produced a flashlight, a comb, some loose change, a couple of crumpled pound notes, a folded scrap of paper, a handkerchief, and a tightly rolled cloth bundle. He laid out his finds on the Headmaster's desk.

Dan unfolded the piece of paper. It contained a sketchmap of the school and grounds, with the Headmaster's study clearly marked. He unrolled the bundle.

It was a long strip of cloth divided into pockets, rather like the larger version of the travel sewing kit for carrying needles and thread. But this kit held a variety of tools, including a drill, several small crowbars, hacksaws and files, and a set of skeleton keys. "The complete burglar's do-it-yourself kit," murmured Dan. "You certainly came well prepared."

"Shall I dial nine-nine-nine?" asked Mickey excitedly.

"Not yet." Dan looked hard at their sullen prisoner. "Look, if we do call the police, you're in big trouble. Burglar's tools, a map. But we're not all that interested in you. We want to know who's behind this, and all the other robberies."

"We want Mr. Big," said Mickey in his tough voice.

"Tell us who it is, and we'll let you go," said Dan persuasively. "They needn't even know we got you. You can go back and say there was nothing here. There isn't, you know—we made that story up just to catch you."

"No cash?"

"There might be a few pounds lunch money, some-where, but that'd be all."

"But Fagin said—" The prisoner stopped himself.

Still in the same quiet voice, Dan said, "Fagin?"

"He just calls himself Fagin. Sort of a joke."

"Tell us his real name then. Just the name and we'll let you go."

"May I inquire what is going on here, Robinson?" An all-too-familiar figure was standing in the doorway. It was the Headmaster—popularly known in the school as Old Fusspot.

Everyone turned in astonishment, and the prisoner seized his chance. With a savage jerk he freed himself from their grip, streaked across the room, and disappeared through the open window.

Jeff shot off after him like a dog after a rabbit. Dan was just about to follow when the Headmaster said, "Just a minute, Robinson. Will you kindly tell me what is happening?"

"We thought this rumor about the money might attract a burglar, sir, so we decided to lie in wait." He thought it more tactful not to mention that they'd started the rumor theselves.

The Headmaster chewed the ragged ends of his mustache, a habit when he was worried—which was most of the time. "I kept thinking about that ridiculous story myself. I had a sudden impulse to come here and check up. And it's just as well I did."

Mickey glared at him. Didn't the old twit realize that if he hadn't turned up, they'd still have their prisoner, and quite likely the name of his boss as well? Dan gave Mickey a warning glance. "We're very grateful for your help, sir," said Dan hurriedly. "But I think we ought to go and see if—"

He broke off as Jeff climbed panting through the window. "Lost him," he gasped. "I got around the corner and there was no sign of him. I heard a car, though. Maybe someone picked him up."

The Headmaster, a bit of a ditherer at the best of things, was now in a state of total confusion. His sacred office full of children, people jumping in and out of the window. . . . He made an attempt to be decisive. "I shall phone the police immediately."

"It's all a bit of a non-event, isn't it, sir?" said Dan gently. "I mean there's no money, no burglary, and now there isn't even a burglar. We'd have to wait for the police to arrive and hang about for ages answering questions . . ."

The Headmaster thought longingly about his favorite armchair. And there was a documentary on Ancient Greece on Channel 2. "Perhaps you're right, Robinson. We'll simply treat the whole incident as closed. Heaven knows the police have enough to worry about without our troubling them with petty vandalism."

"I'm sure you're right, sir," said Dan soothingly. He gave a quick nod to Mickey, who hurriedly swept the evidence they'd taken from the prisoner into his school-bag.

The Headmaster led the way toward the door. "And in future, Robinson, I should be grateful if you would keep your detection off the school premises. I know you managed to score one success in the past, but you mustn't let it go to your head. These matters are far better left to the police, you know."

"Yes, sir, I'm sure you're right, sir," said Dan. The Headmaster led the way out of the school, locked up behind them, and drove away.

As his rear lights disappeared around the corner, Mickey said disgustedly, "Yes, sir, no, sir, three bags full, sir. The silly old twerp ruined everything."

"I think Dan handled him very well," said Liz. "If he hadn't soothed him down we'd have spent half the night answering daft questions from the police—and from our parents."

Although it was late they decided to go around to Dan's for a conference. As Mickey pointed out, it had the advantage of making the story they'd told their parents turn out to be true after all. Dan's mother was out and he made cocoa and sandwiches in the big kitchen. The evidence lay spread before them on the table.

Jeff looked at the pile of odds and ends. "Not much to show for all that waiting, is it?"

"Oh, I don't know," said Dan. "We learned quite a bit tonight."

Liz looked surprised. "Did we? What, for example?"

"Well, for a start, we got confirmation of our theory. The robberies are being carried out by kids, with someone else organizing them."

"I don't know if you could call it confirmation . . ."

"You all saw our burglar. I'm not really sure how old he is, but he was no adult. Next the map. Advance planning and preparation. And finally these." Dan tapped the roll of tools. "They look like professional tools to me—and your average kid doesn't carry stuff like that around."

"Maybe his dad's a burglar too," suggested Mickey. "Family business."

"Finally, there's what the burglar actually said. 'Calls himself Fagin.' Calls himself, you notice. So it's someone educated enough to know about *Oliver Twist* and about Fagin leading a gang of child thieves."

"Everyone knows about Fagin," protested Mickey. "I

saw the film on telly." He began loping about the kitchen singing "You gotta pick a pocket or two!" in a high-pitched whine.

Jeff said, "That increases your suspect list by about ten million or so. I mean, if even Mickey's heard of Fagin . . ."

"I still think I'm right," said Dan obstinately. "Someone's getting hold of kids like that poor little scruff we caught tonight, and organizing them. He probably keeps most of the stolen money for himself, pays them with a few quid."

"And we nearly got his name," said Liz bitterly. "If Old Fusspot hadn't turned up. . . . Now we've lost the name, and the burglar too."

"We've still got his stuff, remember. Maybe that'll tell us something."

Dan began turning over the pile of objects on the table. "Nothing that'd identify him, like a diary or wallet. He'd be sure to leave all that behind. Now, let's see, comb, coins, handkerchief . . . hang on, there's something wrapped in the handkerchief."

He shook the handkerchief and something rolled onto the table and dropped to the floor, where it bounced with a series of diminishing clicks. "A Ping-Pong ball!"

Jeff shrugged. "All right, so he's a keen table-tennis player. That narrows it down to another million or so!"

Dan picked up the ball and examined it. Jeff watched him skeptically. "Unless, of course, that happens to be a rare handmade table-tennis ball, supplied only to one millionaire client?"

"No such luck. It's not the ball itself that tells us something, it's the fact that it was there."

"I don't see what, Dan," said Liz. "Nearly everyone can play table tennis."

"Ah, but only a fairly keen player would carry a ball around. And where does he play?"

"Could be anywhere."

"Could it? How many people have a proper table at home? Where did you learn to play, Jeff? Where is it you can never find a ball when you want one?"

"Youth club," said Jeff. "Balls are always getting lost or trodden on, and the club office never has enough, or it's locked or something. Table-tennis balls are like gold . . ."

"That's right. In a youth club. What better place to find a lot of kids?"

Fagin shoved his companion into the little office, thrust him into a chair and perched on the edge of the desk. "Now for the last time, Rattray, I want the truth. What happened at that school?"

"I told you, there was nothing there. No money, not even a safe. So I just come away, didn't I?"

Fagin nodded to the tall, skinny youth by the door. "Neville says you shot into the car at top speed and yelled at him to step on it. He says you were shaking like a leaf."

"Well, I was nervous, wasn't I?"

"You're an old hand, Ratty. A quick in and out with no trouble wouldn't upset you like that. *So what happened?* I have to know, you see. We don't want to have to get nasty about it, do we? You know I can't stand violence, can I, Bill?"

The massive figure slouched forward. "You want me to duff 'im up a bit?"

"All right, all right," said Rattray disgustedly. "It was a setup. They was waiting for me."

"Police?"

"No, not the law. These kids." He gave a hurried account of his capture and escape.

"And they offered to let you go if you talked? Only you wouldn't talk, would you, Ratty, old friend?"

" 'Course not," said Rattray indignantly. "I told you. This other old geezer came in and I could get away."

"And you're sure he called one of them Robinson?"

"I told you . . ." Rattray made an attempt to imitate the Headmaster's fruity tones: "I say, what's going on here, Robinson?"

Fagin jerked his head toward the door. "All right. Out."

"Don't I get nothing?"

"You didn't fetch anything, did you? Nothing for me, nothing for you."

"All right." Rattray paused by the door. "Give us a new table tennis ball?"

"I gave you one yesterday."

Rattray paused. "Got trod on, didn't it? Come on, one lousy ball . . ."

Fagin took a ball from the box on the desk and tossed it. Rattray caught it neatly and hurried from the room.

Fagin rose and stretched. "Dan Robinson," he said thoughtfully.

"Had his name in the local paper just a while ago," growled Sikes. "Robinson and his Baker Street Irregulars. Gang of kids, playing detective . . ."

"That's right. But don't underestimate them, Bill. They got that painting back, remember."

"So what do we do?"

"I'm afraid you'll have to find young Master Robinson and deliver a little warning . . ."

# 6

# The Warning

Dan knew there was something wrong the minute he turned into his street. It took him a moment to work out what it was—then he realized. Baskerville wasn't in his usual position outside the front door.

It had proved quite a problem when they'd first got the enormous dog. Dan's father was out at work all day, and often away on business trips, his social-worker mother had to go to meetings at all hours, Dan himself had to go to school. Baskerville was a sociable sort of dog, and he didn't much care for being in the house alone. The first time they'd tried it he'd howled dismally for hours, deep, throbbing howls, like wolves howling on the prairie.

In between the howling, Baskerville had dashed up

and down the house out of sheer boredom, overturning chairs, tables, and ornaments in the process. Dan's mother had returned to angry neighbors and a wrecked house. For a while it seemed they'd either have to get rid of Baskerville altogether or hire a full time dogsitter. Then Dan had suggested they try leaving Baskerville in the backyard. They could leave a supply of food and water, and leave the bike shed open for shelter in case of rain.

They tried it. When Dan came home from school, Baskerville was nowhere in sight. He'd got bored with the limited attractions of the garden, opened the back gate with his nose, and wandered off. Dan was just about to go and report a lost dog to the police station when Baskerville ambled into the kitchen, sitting hopefully by his dog bowl.

"Better let him do as he likes," said Dan's father. "He's a dog that knows his own mind."

From then on Baskerville lived a life of total freedom. When there was no one at home he ambled up and down the street or sat on the front steps watching life go by.

He was a firm favorite with all the local toddlers, there were dog friends in the street to pass the time of day with, and he soon discovered that if he went into one of the local shops and barked, they'd give him a sweet or a cookie to go away. Dan's father said Baskerville was the only dog in the world who ran a protection racket.

Sometimes Dan felt that the street owned Baskerville as much as he did. The dog was a sort of community asset, like the mail box, or the telephone booth on the corner. But Baskerville was always waiting on the corner of the street when it was time for Dan to come home from school—he seemed to have some sort of internal clock—and by the way he hurled himself upon Dan, it was easy to see that he had only been passing time until Dan got home.

As all these thoughts flashed through his mind, Dan realized immediately what was wrong. No Baskerville. The dog wasn't hurtling toward him, as he did most days. He wasn't even sitting on the steps in a lordly fashion, as he did in his dignified moods. He just wasn't there.

Puzzled, Dan went on toward the house. He'd planned to take Baskerville for a walk right after school—or rather a bike ride for Dan and a run for Baskerville. No normal walk was enough to exercise the enormous dog, so Dan usually rode his bike all around the edge of the local park while Baskerville loped happily beside him. Dan turned down the narrow side passage that led to the backyard. With a feeling of relief he saw Baskerville stretched out in front of the bike shed. Then the relief started fading away. Baskerville was lying too still for sleep. . . . Inside the open shed Dan could see his bike—or what was left of it. It was a twisted metal wreck. Wheels and handlebars had been wrenched from the frame and stamped into unrecognizable shapes. Even the lamps had been carefully stamped into fragments of metal and glass.

The bike was one of Dan's most precious possessions,

but he hardly glanced at it. He knelt down beside Baskerville. The big dog was lying completely still, and the fur on top of his head was matted and stiff with blood. Dan put a hand on the dog's flank. It was moving up and down, ever so slightly, and he thought he could feel the faintest whisper of a heartbeat. Dan remembered there was a vet about three streets away. His office must be about due to open. He lifted the dog with an effort—Baskerville was almost as heavy as a man—and carried him through the streets to the vet's office, through the waiting room, and laid him on the vet's table.

Luckily the vet was a sensible man. He shooed away the cat-owning old lady who was insisting it was her Fluffie's turn next, and started to examine Baskerville.

Dan stood waiting as the vet felt the dog's skull. Then he looked up. "I think he's just been knocked out. The skull doesn't seem to be broken. . . . There's a risk of concussion, though—I won't be able to tell much till he comes around. I'd better keep him here."

The vet's assistant was a girl not much older than Dan, and between them they carried Baskerville through to the animal hospital behind the surgery. They settled him in the biggest basket in the place, and the girl began bathing his bruised head. "How did it happen?"

"We had a burglar. He must have hit him with some kind of club."

"You'd think a dog this size could tackle anyone."

"The thing is, he's too trusting. Thinks everybody's his friend." For a moment Dan felt like crying, which was ridiculous at his age. He arranged to telephone for news later, and went around to the police station.

Detective Constable Day said sympathetically, "Poor old Baskerville. Be all right, will he?"

"I hope so. They're not quite sure yet." Dan spoke with a frozen calm.

"He'll pull through all right. I'll have to call around and take him a bunch of bones!" Day paused. "Nasty business, the bike smashed and all. Wonder why they picked on you?"

"I think I can tell you that—it was a warning." Dan told him about the trap in the school and the burglar who'd got away.

"You reckon you're on to something, and they're trying to frighten you off?"

"What else could it be? There was no damage anywhere else in the street. I checked."

"And you think it's someone organizing kids using a youth club for a front? That's putting quite a lot on just one Ping-Pong ball."

"It fits though, doesn't it? How's the crime wave?"

"Dropping off. Burglary rates nearly back to normal, but we're having a run on pickpocketing!"

"There can't be much loose cash about by now. They were bound to turn to something else."

Day looked thoughtfully at him. "Hang on a minute." He left his office and disappeared down the corridor. A few minutes later he was back. "I checked with WPC Lee, the Juvenile Officer."

"And?"

"She says juvenile crime is down over the last few weeks. Some of her best customers seem to be reforming."

"That fits too, doesn't it? Maybe they've found something more profitable to do."

"You don't give up, do you, young Robinson? All right, what do you want me to do?"

"A bit of advice for a start. If you wanted to recruit a lot of criminal kids, where would you go?"

"The Estate," said Day promptly. "Top spot for vandalism, muggings, handbag snatching, shop robberies, and car thefts in the entire area. Half the kids around there cut their teeth on a burglar's jimmy."

Dan nodded thoughtfully. He knew all about the Estate from his mother, who said it was the biggest social scandal in the area.

It had been one of the earliest tower-block developments in London: now it was one of the oldest and most run down, a scattering of grimy gray towers with windy concrete plazas in between—no shops, no cinemas, no pubs.

By the time everyone finally realized that people from small, friendly streets didn't actually like living in little boxes in the sky, the Estate was already on the decline. Everyone who could manage it moved out as soon as he could, and now the only ones left were those who hadn't managed to get away. Embarrassed by the number of vacancies, the housing authorities had used the Estate to house what they called problem families, concentrating all the troublemakers in one place. Now the whole place had degenerated into a kind of instant slum, with shabby-looking buildings, lifts that never worked, and grimy rubble-strewn staircases covered with spray-can graffiti. Nobody went near the Estate now, except those who had to because they still lived there, and even the police were careful to go in pairs.

"It doesn't sound like much of a place for youth clubs," said Dan thoughtfully. "Are there many?"

"You'd be surprised. Just recently everyone realized the Estate was a problem, and now the social workers are starting to outnumber the villains. There's that new Civic Sports Center for a start . . ."

Conscious that the Estate had been neglected, the housing authorities had tried to make amends by building a magnificent new recreation center close by. There was a swimming pool, and facilities for every sport you could think of—squash, basketball, tennis. No doubt there was a table-tennis room as well.

"That's a bit big," said Dan. "A smaller place would be easier for them to control. Do you think you could get me a list of youth clubs in the area? And run a discreet check on whoever's in charge?"

Day sighed. He got up and went out of the office again, returning a few minutes later with a faded carbon-copy list which he passed to Dan. "Let's have it back when you've finished with it."

Dan stood up. "You'll let me know if you turn up anyone suspicious?"

"All right. Don't suppose I will, though, those people are usually checked out pretty carefully before they get the job." He paused. "I don't suppose it's any use telling you to stay out of this?"

"After what they did to Baskerville?"

"That's what I thought. Be careful. Next time it could be your head that gets bashed."

Later that evening Dan told a shocked meeting of the Irregulars what had happened to Baskerville. Luckily there was good news as well. He had just visited Baskerville at the animal hospital, and the vet seemed to think there would be no permanent damage. Baskerville had been woozy from an injection, and there had been a bandage on his head. But he'd opened his eyes at the sound of Dan's voice, and had even managed to lick his hand. "I'm really going after these people now," concluded Dan grimly. "Of course I'd like your help—but I warn you it could be dangerous. As Day said, it could be one of us next time."

"Of course we'll all help," said Liz fiercely. "And if I get hold of whoever hit Baskerville . . ."

Jeff and Mickey were just as eager. "What are we going to do?" asked Jeff.

"We'll check this list of youth clubs. Just turn up, say we're thinking of joining, and have a look around. Keep an eye out for the kid we caught in the study. He's our only real contact. If we spot him . . ."

"Where do we start?"

"With the new Sports Center . . ."

After a short train journey—it was one stop on the Underground—they arrived at the new Sports Center. It was a low, sprawling affair in white concrete, and it looked incongruously clean amidst the grimy towers that surrounded it.

They went up the steps and into the foyer. It was huge and round, with plastic oak paneling. Doors led off to the various activities, and a white stone staircase led to the upper floors. The place was packed, and the air was full of the noise of various sporting activities—echoing shouts from a swimming pool and the steady tock-tock-tock of squash balls, and the shuffle of sneakered feet from the basketball hall.

There was a ticket office at the back of the foyer, with a small door beside it. Dan was just about to go over and ask if they could look around when a tall, fair-haired young man in a denim suit came out. He looked curiously at them for a moment and said, "Hello, it's young Robinson, isn't it, our local Sherlock Holmes?"

Dan groaned, wondering who this dressed-up idiot was. The last thing he wanted was people shouting his name about. But he forced himself to smile and said politely, "That's right. Do we know each other?"

"Well, not really. I recognized you from your picture in the local paper. I used to go to your school, but you were younger then. . . . The name's Vosper, Chris Vosper." He held out his hand.

Dan took it, conscious that he was shaking hands with a legend, or at the very best an ex-legend. Chris Vosper had been a school celebrity. Not only was he Head of Games, Head Prefect, and team captain or star player in almost every sport, he was also supposed to be brilliant academically. He'd already got a place at Oxford on interview, and he was going to take it up as soon as he

collected enough "A" levels. On top of all this he was
the only son of a millionaire business tycoon, with a seat
on the board of the family business waiting for him.

Then suddenly he'd chucked it all up, leaving school
just before his "A" levels and disappearing.

"So this is where you got to!" said Dan curiously.

"Well—not right away! I did go around the world
first!"

It was Mickey who asked the question in all their
minds. "Why did you just disappear like that?"

Liz jabbed him in the ribs. "Mind your own business,
Mickey."

Chris smiled, and it was clear his famous charm was as
strong as ever. "It's all right, it's a natural question." He
looked around the little group. "I don't know if you're
old enough to understand, though. The thing is, it
suddenly seemed a bit too easy, a bit *too* well planned.
School, Oxford, taking over from Dad. . . . I could see
my entire life a nice smooth highway stretching ahead. I
wanted to go down a few byways first. So I grew long
hair and a beard and went off to Katmandu!"

Mickey looked at the immaculate figure before them.
"You don't look very hippie now."

"Well, I got it all out of my system. I knocked about a
bit, did all sorts of jobs, came home by way of Australia,
worked my way back through Europe, made it up with
the old man, and here I am!"

"What are you doing now?" asked Liz.

"I'm going to take a social-work course, do a bit of
good in the world. Dad still wanted me in the business,
but he came around. Meanwhile I help out here for a bit

of practical experience . . ." He broke off. "Listen, you don't want my boring life story—what are you all doing here? Are you on a case? I read about that painting business . . ."

Mickey opened his mouth and shut it again when Dan trod heavily on his toe. Dan said, "We just thought we'd take a look around, see what was here."

"There's everything here," said Chris proudly. "You name it, we've got it. Swimming, basketball, squash, judo, fencing, boxing, weight lifting . . ."

"What about table tennis?"

"Table-tennis room just up the stairs. Tables are pretty busy, though . . ."

A couple of lads were coming down the stairs arguing. "Just because you had a lucky game," one of them was saying.

The other laughed. "Luck! That was sheer science. I smashed you right off the table . . ."

He had a high-pitched nasal voice that was very familiar. Dan swung around. The boy coming down the stairs was the burglar they'd caught in the Headmaster's study.

# 7

---

# Ambush

At the sight of the little group of Irregulars, a look of utter astonishment filled the boy's face.

"Hey, you!" shouted Dan. But he was already too late. Moving with the same ratlike speed he'd shown in the playground, the boy darted down the steps, across the foyer, and out of the front door. He shot off so fast he dropped his racket on the stairs, but he didn't stop for it.

Dan was after him in a flash, the others close behind. They were in time to see him disappear around the corner, and they all dashed after him. Their quarry ran down the side of the building and vanished behind it.

At the rear of the Sports Center was the parking lot, a dimly lit cinder-covered yard with a high wire fence around it. They were just in time to see the boy streak between the cars and climb up the wire fence like a monkey. He scrambled over the top and disappeared into the darkness of the waste ground beyond.

Jeff had a go at climbing the fence, but he was too heavy and it buckled beneath his weight. Mickey was already halfway up when Dan tapped him on the back. "Come on down, Mickey, it's too late now. He's on his home ground here."

Reluctantly Mickey came down.

As they walked back across the parking lot, Liz said, "Well, that proves you were right, doesn't it, Dan?"

"That's right," said Mickey eagerly. "The burglary racket must be run from here."

Dan wasn't sure. "I still think this place is too big. Things would be difficult to control. Too many people would have to be in the know. After all, there's no reason he couldn't be going to more than one youth club."

"Still, it's a start, isn't it?" said Jeff. "What do we do now?"

"We'll take a look around here, and then split up and tackle the smaller clubs. You never know, we might see our friend again."

Chris Vosper was waiting for them in the foyer. "What was all that about?"

"Just someone we wanted to see," said Dan evasively. "I don't suppose you happen to know who he was?"

"Not one of our regulars . . ." He turned to the other boy, who was still hanging about. "You were playing with him, you must know who he was."

The boy shrugged. "Never seen him before tonight.

He's a good player, but he's such a loudmouth no one wants to play with him." He went off to the canteen.

Chris was looking quizzically at them. "I won't ask you what all this is about. Another case, I suppose?" He picked up the dropped racket. It was oddly shaped, and covered with thick sponge rubber on either side. "Doesn't stint himself on his bats, whoever he is. Latest Chinese-type model this is, cost a bundle. I've got one myself." He put the racket inside the little office. "I'll hang on to this. If he comes back to claim it I'll see if I can get a name out of him." He closed the door. "Look, I'm finishing my stint soon, but I've got time to show you around if you like."

"Are you sure?" said Liz. "We don't want to be a nuisance."

"My pleasure." He led the way up the stairs. "Now on my left we have the magnificently appointed table-tennis room . . ."

Chris took them all over the enormous building, swimming pool, squash courts, three different gymnasiums used for judo and basketball, and even a room for chess and dominoes.

The place was packed with cheerful, noisy kids of all ages. Dan recognized quite a few from his own school. In one of the gyms there was a basketball match in progress, with parents cheering the players on from the spectators' gallery. The more they saw, the more Dan became convinced the whole place was too big and too complex to be the front for any sort of criminal enterprise.

They finished up in the canteen, having a cup of

tea—or rather a cup of tea and several Cokes, with Mr. Jamieson, the Director of the Sports Center, a gloomy, harassed man with thinning fair hair, who seemed to have a grudge against life.

Tactfully Dan said, "I get the impression you don't get too many really local kids in here."

Jamieson nodded sadly. "It's always the way. You build a place like this to serve a deprived area, and who turns up? Kids from good homes, like yourselves. Fair enough, the place is here, why shouldn't you use it? But the ones who really need help, the real delinquents— nine times out of ten they just don't come in."

"Maybe they'd sooner steal cars than play basketball?" suggested Mickey. Tact had never been his strong point.

"Do you ever get any of the tougher kids?" asked Liz.

Chris shrugged. "There were one or two about when I first came; in fact, we had quite a few troublemakers. I showed 'em we wouldn't stand any nonsense and they drifted off again."

"Where do they go?" asked Dan.

"No idea. I suppose they went back to hanging around street corners. There are plenty of youth clubs in the area; maybe they prefer one of them."

Perhaps they do, thought Dan—and it was time he started looking for it. He finished his Coke. "I think we'd better be on our way. We'll have a look at some of the other clubs and meet back here."

Chris stood up. "I'll see you out then. I'm off myself now."

Chris insisted on paying for the Cokes and tea, and

they made their way out to the parking lot, where he opened the door of a big white sports car.

Mickey stared at it in admiration. "Here, that's a Lamborghini, isn't it?"

"That's right. Picked her up in Rome and drove her home." He turned to Dan. "I won't ask what you are up to—but if I can be of any help, all you've got to do is ask. Maybe I can be a fifth Irregular."

"Thanks, we'll keep it in mind."

Chris waved his hand, and the sports car roared away.

There were ten names altogether on the list, and with the Sports Center already covered, that left nine to go. Dan had it all worked out. "Jeff can take the first three, Mickey and Liz do the next three together, and I'll take the last three. We'll all meet back here when we're finished. If anyone finds anything suspicious, we'll all four go and check it tomorrow night."

There was a bit of argument about Liz and Mickey being paired, but Dan solved it by giving both of them the impression they were looking after the other. Besides, he pointed out, how else could you divide nine places between four people? Before leaving home Dan had prepared three lists, each holding three names, with a sketch map attached, drawn up from his A to Z. He handed one to Jeff, one to Liz, and kept the third for himself. They set off on their separate journeys.

A couple of hours later Dan was groping his way along a dark, deserted street, looking for the third name on his list.

He'd started with the most distant club so as to be

working his way back toward the Center. He'd found the place easily enough, it was in a church hall on a main road. It had been Cub Scout night, and the place had been full of green-capped kids playing complicated team games and struggling with reef knots and wrapping each other up in bandages till they looked like mummies. The leader had told Dan there was a club for young teenagers, but it wasn't open until the next night.

Making a note to check the place tomorrow, Dan had gone on to the next address. He'd found that one easily too, although it was in a back street. It was dance and disco night, and the ground was vibrating with the noise for miles around. Inside the place had been packed with leaping teenagers, and Dan's brief conversation with the club leader had been held at the top of his voice. He was an enormous young curate, a perfect example of muscular Christianity.

"They're a good crowd," he roared, "just a shade noisy. No, we don't get any troublemakers. We used to, but I cuffed a few and they seem to have stopped coming."

Dan struggled to the exit, narrowly escaping the clutches of a plump girl with purple hair who seemed to have taken a fancy to him. Thankfully he staggered out into the fresh air, though his ears went on ringing until he was several streets away.

So his first two attempts hadn't been very encouraging, and now he couldn't find the third place at all. According to his own sketch map, the place should have been somewhere at the end of this street. But the street itself was dark and silent. Most of the buildings seemed to be shabby offices or little warehouses, and they nearly all had their windows boarded up. The street itself was a blind alley, ending in a bricked-up archway beneath the railway bridge that blocked the end.

It wasn't until he got to the very end of the street that Dan found what he was looking for. There was a padlocked wooden door in the wall across the railway arch and a faded painted notice read "St. George's Youth Club." Dan tugged at the huge rusty padlock, but it held fast. Disappointed, he turned away. "First Cub Scouts, then disco dancers, then nobody," he thought. Perhaps the others had had better luck.

It was later than he'd expected by the time he got back, and the Sports Center was closing. Mr. Jamieson was in the foyer, shooing the last few kids out and getting ready to lock up. "Haven't seen any sign of your friends," he said. "They're not in here anyway, I'm just about to lock up. Try the parking lot."

Dan asked about the closed-down youth club, and Mr. Jamieson laughed. "St. George's? Could have saved you a trip if you'd asked me. That used to be the main club for the Estate. Nearest one, you see. I used to work there myself. When this place opened up, they closed it down. It's been closed for over a year. Whole area's coming down." Mr. Jamieson smiled almost nostalgically. "My word, that was a dump. Plenty of space, mind you, there's miles of room under that arch, and a big yard at the back. But talk about dark and gloomy . . . and my word, we used to get some tough customers . . ." He told Dan a long sad story about a trusted assistant who had to be dismissed for theft.

"He'd actually been keeping the stolen goods in the club. He had to go, of course. Took it very badly. . . . Still, I mustn't hang about chatting. Got to check the day's take before I go home."

Dan hung about on the steps for a while, and then decided to go and look around the back of the building. Perhaps when he'd said, "meet back here" they'd thought he meant the exact spot on which they'd all parted. There was only one car in the parking lot, a battered old Ford, presumably waiting to take Mr. Jamieson home.

It was dark now, and outside the circle of light cast by the single streetlamp at the back of the building, the parking lot was gloomy and shadowed.

Dan decided that it would be a lot more cheerful waiting on the front steps, and turned to go back to the front of the building. A voice spoke out of the shadows. "Dan Robinson?"

"That's right."

"Some people just won't take a friendly warning," said the voice.

"Is that what you call smashing up my bike, and half killing my dog?" Dan went on walking at the same steady pace. If he could reach the streetlamp. . . .

"Still had to go poking your nose in," said the muffled voice. "Now you're going to finish up like the dog—in the hospital. Maybe they'll put you in the next bed."

Dan made a sudden dart for the gate, but he was too late. A massive black-clad figure appeared out of the darkness, barring his way. To his horror, Dan saw that it had no face. . . .

# 8

# The Fight

The figure wasn't really faceless. It was wearing black
leather motorcycle gear, complete with helmet. Under
the helmet was a stocking-mask, and the man's features
were blurred and distorted by the nylon. Funny how
such an everyday object could turn an ordinary face into
something out of a nightmare.

While these random thoughts flashed through Dan's
mind, he was sizing up his opponent. He was both taller
and broader than Dan, and looked to be very strong.
But size and strength aren't everything. . . .

"You know you're in trouble," said Dan conversation-
ally. "Stupid trying this sort of thing here. People are
going by all the time, and the place is too well lit."

"Maybe we can alter that," said the voice. A half-brick whizzed out of the darkness, and the streetlamp went out in a shower of flying glass.

So his attacker wasn't alone, and now the whole parking lot was in semidarkness. There was still a chance, though. If he could get away before they closed in on him. . . .

"That's just about your mark," said Dan scornfully. "Chucking stones at streetlights! Why don't you make a run for it before the policeman comes?"

With a roar of anger his attacker rushed him. Dan made no attempt to dodge. Instead he caught hold of the lapels of the leather jacket and threw himself backward. Carried by the force of his own charge, his attacker fell forward on top of him. Still using his attacker's momentum, Dan rolled over backward, shoved both feet in the man's middle, and straightened his legs. . . . It was a classic judo throw, and his opponent flew a surprising distance through the air before landing with a bone-shaking thud on the cinder-packed ground.

Dan rolled over onto his feet. A throw like that can leave the victim incapable, if not actually unconscious. Now was his chance to make a run for it. . . .

But no sooner had he taken the first step when his arms were grabbed from behind. "We've got him," shouted an exultant voice in his ear. "You all right, Sikesy?"

The massive figure on the ground stirred. "Hold him," it said. "Just hold him till I get up."

Dan struggled wildly, but there were two of his new opponents, one to each arm. The man on the ground got painfully to his feet and lumbered toward them. The heavy motorcycle boots crunched on the cinders. "Hold him," said the slurred voice again, and one of those boots drew back for a kick. Dan found himself watching the huge scarred toecap in helpless fascination. . . .

A stocky figure hurtled across the parking lot and launched itself across through the air in a flying tackle that was almost parallel to the ground. Jeff was one of the best Rugby players in the school, and the big man, who was standing on one foot anyway, went down for the second time, hitting his head against the front bumper of the old Ford.

The two lads holding Dan slackened their grip with surprise, and with a sudden twist he wrenched himself free. Swinging around he abandoned judo for a thump on the ear that sent his nearest opponent staggering back with a yell of pain.

Jeff was dealing with the other attacker by now. He dodged a windmilling fist with ease, feinted with his right, and landed a really satisfying straight left bang on the nose. The attacker fell back, his hands to his face—and more dark figures came out of the shadows. Dan and Jeff stood back to back ready to fight off their shadowy attackers. The huge figure on the ground was already struggling to its feet. . . .

Liz and Mickey saw the group of struggling figures as they ran into the parking lot. Liz was able to look after herself in any playground scuffle, but she knew it would be sheer stupidity to plunge into a fight like this. She grabbed Mickey's collar—he was just about to hurl himself into the fray—and shouted, "Mickey, go to the Sports Center and hammer on the door till they let you in. Get them to call the police. I'll see if there's anyone going by on the road!"

They turned and ran, Mickey up the steps, Liz into the road that ran past the Center. She stood in the middle of the road looking up and down. But it was that curiously slack midpart of the evening, neither early nor late, and there just didn't seem to be any traffic around.

A white shape skidded around the corner and zoomed toward her. Liz jumped up and down waving her arms. "Chris!" she yelled. "Chris Vosper!" The car skidded to a halt beside her and Chris looked out. "Still here?" he said chattily. "I was all set to go to the theater then I found I'd left the tickets here. My date will be furious. Hey, what's up?"

"Parking lot!" gasped Liz. "Dan and Jeff . . ."

"Are they hurt? Get in!"

Liz jumped into the passenger seat and the car swung around the corner and into the parking lot, its headlights illuminating a group of wildly struggling figures. Chris leaped out of the car, and Liz jammed her finger on the horn and kept it there. The parking lot was filled with the shattering high-pitched howl of the Klaxon.

Panic-stricken, most of the attackers turned and ran, disappearing into the darkness. Chris squared up to the giant in motorcycle gear, though with rather more enthusiasm than skill. He slammed a wild punch into the man's middle, but the blow caught the heavy buckle on the motorcycle jacket and did more harm to Chris's fist than to his opponent. For a moment the motorcyclist stared at this new attacker in almost comical surprise. Then he swung one arm like a flail in a blow that knocked Chris clear off his feet and ran to the back of the parking lot. There was the roar of an engine and seconds later he reappeared astride an enormous motorbike, narrowly missing Mr. Jamieson, who'd been summoned at last by Mickey's frantic knocking.

Liz had got out of the car and was helping Chris to his feet. He rubbed his aching head. "So much for Saint George to the rescue! I think you'd better tackle him next time, Liz."

"You got rid of him for us all the same," said Dan seriously. "We could have managed the smaller ones, but he was like King Kong!"

Chris grinned. "You'll have to make me an honorary Irregular after all."

Mr. Jamieson came puffing up and Dan told him they'd spotted a gang of vandals smashing a streetlamp and been attacked when they tried to stop them. It was a nice simple story, and one the police would accept. Mr. Jamieson promised to report it immediately and he and Chris went back into the Center. Battered but jubilant, the Irregulars set off home.

It was a triumphant meeting in Dan's room later that evening. For one thing, Dan's mother had had a message from the vet. Baskerville had made a good recovery with no complications, and he would come home soon. For another, they had beaten off their attackers and emerged more or less victorious.

"All the same it's a good thing Chris turned up," said Liz.

"So it's Chris now, is it," teased Mickey. "Well, your

dreamboat didn't show up too well when it came to it, did he? Could have done better myself!''

Liz aimed a clout at his ear, and Dan said, ''He'd have swatted you like a fly, Mickey. And Liz is quite right. It was Chris turning up that got us out of real trouble.''

Jeff brought them down to earth. ''We may have avoided getting our blocks knocked off, but we didn't get much further with the investigation.''

They had compared notes on returning to Dan's room, and Jeff, Liz, and Mickey had nothing to report but a series of visits to perfectly ordinary youth clubs, with nothing suspicious about either staff or members.

''There was one thing,'' said Dan. ''The curious business of the suspicious characters.''

''But there weren't any suspicious characters,'' said Jeff.

''Exactly. That was the curious incident.'' Dan beamed, pleased with this neat paraphrase of one of his favorite Sherlock Holmes remarks. ''Listen, nearly all the clubs we covered between us said they'd had some dodgy members in the past, but they'd all stopped coming.''

Liz frowned. ''That's natural enough. The sort of kid who goes around stealing cars and stealing old ladies' handbags probably doesn't go in much for woodwork classes or table tennis.''

''Why not? Even a villain can get bored. They can't go out breaking and entering every night, even on the Estate. So, where do they go to, eh?''

''Brings us back to your original theory, doesn't it?''

said Jeff. "A special club for villains! It's a nice idea . . . but where is the place—if it exists . . ."

"I know it exists," said Dan fiercely. "It's the only theory that fits all the facts."

"When you have eliminated the impossible," said Liz solemnly, "then what remains, *however improbable, must be the truth!*"

Dan looked up in surprise, and Liz grinned. She'd been reading up on her Sherlock Holmes since the formation of the Irregulars.

"Exactly," said Dan when he'd recovered from the shock of Liz's apt quotation. "Logically speaking, the place *must* exist. All we've got to do is find it!"

"Shouldn't be all that hard to find a youth club," said Jeff. "I mean, it's a lot bigger than a painting . . ."

"Well, it wasn't any of those places we visited tonight," said Mickey positively. He wasn't a great fan of youth clubs. "They were about as sinister as a vicarage tea party. I doubt if any of 'em'd so much as fiddle the raffle tickets, let alone rob a safe . . ."

Dan scratched his nose. "We'll just have to check them all again, I suppose . . ." He stopped, staring as if in fascination at his own finger.

Mickey thought he'd cracked up. "What're you doing, hypnotizing yourself?"

Dan went on staring absorbedly at his fingers. "I've got oil on my hands."

"You should wash them then," said Liz bossily.

"The thing is, where did it come from?"

Dan stared wildly at them. "I'll tell you where it came

from. I tried the padlock on that youth club that was closed."

Liz looked blankly at him. "So? People do oil padlocks."

"The place has been shut down for over a year," shouted Dan. "No one ever goes there anymore. The whole street is scheduled for demolition. So—how come that great rusty old padlock is dripping with oil?"

"There could be lots of explanations," said Liz.

"That's right," said Dan. "And mine is the most likely. That place is perfect—right in the middle of an area cleared for demolition, not a soul for miles."

"You mean Jamieson?" asked Jeff incredulously. "He's not my idea of a Moriarty."

"It could be Jamieson," said Dan. "He used to work there. Or . . ." Something was coming back to him. "When we were chatting earlier, he told me a tale about some assistant who was using the place to store stolen goods. They had to sack him."

They all looked at each other. "It's perfect," breathed Liz. "Someone already in youth work, with a criminal record, who knows all about the empty club."

"That's right," added Jeff. "He could easily have hung on to a set of spare keys when he was fired."

Mickey leaned back, hands clasped behind his head. "Well, that's it," he said grandly. "Case solved. Jamieson will tell you this bloke's name tomorrow, you tell your mate Detective Constable Day, he does a bit of checking up, and there you are!"

"This isn't the last five minutes of Kojak, you know," said Dan. "And you know what Day will say—theories and suspicions aren't evidence. Knowing isn't proving. Is there enough information to get a warrant? Will the case stand up in court?"

Jeff sighed. He'd had a feeling it wasn't going to be that easy. "All right. How do we get this evidence?"

"Everything depends on my being right about that empty youth club. And there's only one way to find out. We go and take a look." Dan stood up. "Ready, everybody?"

Liz gasped. "Now?"

"Now," said Dan firmly. "We've already got them worried just by poking around. They might just decide to clear out—and I don't want them to get away."

# 9

# Commando Raid

"Come on," hissed Mickey. "It's dead easy." He swung his legs over the edge of the footbridge and edged his way along the narrow ledge. Cautiously the others followed.

They were attacking the suspected youth club from the rear. As Dan pointed out, the front was hopeless, a narrow alley, no shelter, and a small door in a blank wall. The rear of the building offered far more chance. The main building consisted of the railway arch itself, bricked up at both ends. There was a yard at the back surrounded by high stone walls, and a couple of smaller outbuildings adjoined the yard. It was possible, not easy, but possible, to climb over the edge of the railway footbridge and get onto the top of the wall that ran around the yard.

Mickey had managed it already, and was running along the wall like a cat, while Liz, Dan and Jeff followed more cautiously behind. The wall was topped with broken glass, but sheer old age had worn the points down enough so that it was easy enough to walk on if you were careful.

The wall ended in a flat-roofed building that ran across the back of the little yard. Mickey waited here for the others, and one by one they edged their way across to join him.

At a signal from Dan they all stretched out flat on the roof and studied the scene before them. Below was a square cobbled yard. On the opposite side was the rear wall of the railway-arch building, a door in its center. High stone walls bounded the yard to their left and right. The right-hand wall had a set of huge wooden gates, presumably leading to the street outside.

"The place is like a fortress," whispered Jeff. "Ali Baba and the Forty Thieves could be whooping it up in there for all we'd know."

Dan nodded silently. Unfortunately the back of the building was as secretive as the front. A blank wall, a small door, a couple of high stone windows. The roof of the building was the railway bridge itself, so there was no hope of a skylight or anything like that. The place was perfect for the thieves, if they were using it—and hopeless for the investigators.

Dan sighed, admitting defeat. He'd have to go to Day with just his theory after all and hope the detective would be sufficiently impressed to investigate. He was just about to tell the others to go back when the door in the yard opened with a rumbling sound. A bright-yellow sedan drove in.

"Morris Marina," whispered Mickey instantly. "This year's model too. Very nice!"

A denim-jacketed youth got out of the car and rang the front-door bell beside the door. A second, almost identical youth was closing and locking the wooden doors behind the car.

The door to the building opened and light flooded into the courtyard. A crowd of kids poured out, most of them teenage or just under. They crowded excitedly around the car. There was a babble of approving comment, and several times the two newcomers were congratulated and patted approvingly on the back.

An older man came forward, and the little crowd fell back to make way for him. He was a stocky, anonymous-looking man in a raincoat and flat cap, a cigarette dangling from the corner of his mouth. He walked around the car, nodding approvingly. "Nice, very nice."

"What's happening?" whispered Jeff. "Do you think they've just bought it or something?"

Mickey jabbed him in the ribs. "Just pinched it, more like!"

The cloth-capped man's next words proved that Mickey was right.                                                                      ·

"Now, you all take a lesson from these two lads. Most of you would have come back with a Rolls or a Jag if you had the chance." He shook his head emphatically. "Useless. Too easy to trace, probably loaded up with antithief devices in the first place. No, what you want is a good-class everyday model like this. New license plates, new engine numbers and registration and you've got a guaranteed sale. Now what's better, couple of dozen of these going through with no trouble at all—or one lousy Rolls you'll probably get stuck with anyway?"

"Those oil sheikhs all have 'em," objected a voice.

The man gave him a withering look. "It's a long way to Arabia in a hot jam jar, sonny—and why bother when I can sell this one in Croydon?"

Disposing of his questioner, he turned to the audience. "So, first thing is, pick your model. You'll be given a list of the makes we want. Mind you stick to it." He looked around. "Second, doing the job. Now, how do we get the car away?" Several hands shot up—it was all curiously like school, thought Dan.

The man pointed to the nearest volunteer. "You hot-wire 'em," he said eagerly. "I've seen it on television. You run these leads in the engine, and . . ."

The man cut him off. "How long do you think you'll last fumbling about in some motor with a pair of pliers and a set of crocodile clips? And what do you tell Old Bill if he turns up? You're from the Automobile Association and forgot your uniform?"

There was a ripple of laughter. The man said patiently, "First you get into the car, through the door. And the first thing you do is try it and see if it's open. You'll be surprised how often it is. If it isn't open, you use these." He held up an enormous bunch of keys. "Obtainable from the key counter at your friendly local hardware shop."

There was more laughter.

As the lecture went on, Dan listened in amazement. His fantastic theory was being confirmed beneath his eyes. Here was a night-school course for criminals in full swing.

Dan was so fascinated by all the implications that he didn't really register Mickey's next remark. "I'll just nip down and have a look inside while they're all busy out here."

Dan actually muttered, "Yeah, okay," before the full impact of Mickey's words sank in. Then he hissed urgently, "Mickey, don't be so daft!" But it was too late. Mickey had slipped over the edge of the wall, hung at full length for a moment, and then dropped monkeylike into a dark corner of the yard.

Horrified, but powerless to interfere, Dan saw him creep out of the shadows and sidle round the edge of the attentive crowd. No one seemed to notice him.

Jeff nudged him. "Did you see what I saw? That's Mickey. What does he think he's doing?"

"He's just nipping in to take a look around!" whispered Dan. He blamed himself for not stopping Mickey in time, but it was too late now.

They all watched helplessly as Mickey slipped through the still open door to the main building. "Well, he's in," whispered Liz.

Dan nodded. "The problem now is—how is he going to get out?"

Mickey found himself in a huge whitewashed room with a vaulted roof. Crates and boxes of all kinds were stacked around the walls, many of them with famous brand names stenciled on the side. If the names on the boxes were to be believed, this was as fine a store of color TV sets, hi-fi equipment, furs, whiskey, and cigarettes as you could wish to find. There were tables and benches scattered about the enormous room, and— there was even an old table-tennis table.

On one of the benches stood a safe, the lock partly blown away. A blackboard in the corner showed a large-scale ordnance survey map of a London suburb, with a street-corner bank circled in red, and possible escape routes traced in different-colored inks. Charts on the wall showed different makes of cars, with a price marked beside each model. On another bench there was a pile of two-way radio equipment, some of it partly taken to pieces. Most sinister of all was a kind of armory, with pistols, a sawn-off shotgun, and a variety of clubs. This was in a far corner away from the rest, and a sandbag-padded firing range had been set up beyond it. Mickey saw with astonishment that the life-size target silhouettes were in the shape of policemen. . . .

He wandered around in fascination, keeping to the edges of the room, ready to duck back into cover. His attention was caught by a series of posters showing tough-looking men, and he crossed to examine them. Under a picture of one particularly villainous looking type was written: "Detective Sergeant Tanner, recently transferred from West End Central to the Flying Squad. . . . Frequently works undercover, often armed. Approach with caution, extremely dangerous."

Mickey shook his head in astonishment. It was like a

Police Training College in reverse. He was just thinking it was time to get back to the roof when a suspicious voice said, "Why aren't you out there with the others?"

Mickey turned. There was a kind of bar set up in one corner, loaded with beer and soft-drink cans and cartons of cigarettes. Someone had just popped up from behind it, and was staring at him suspiciously.

Like his idol James Bond, Mickey had his cover story all prepared. He reckoned there was a fair chance they didn't all know each other all that well, and it was his plan to claim that he was a new recruit.

But the sight of the figure behind the bar made him forget his carefully prepared story. It was the ratty-faced boy they'd caught in the Headmaster's study, and almost caught again at the Sports Center. Mickey stared at him openmouthed.

"You'll catch it if they find you skiving off," said the boy. "What you think this is, school or something? Why aren't you outside?"

"Why aren't you?" countered Mickey. To his delight he realized that the other still hadn't recognized him.

The skinny boy sniffed. "Done me basic motoring ages ago, haven't I? I'm just setting up the bar for the break. Haven't seen you before, have I?"

Mickey told his story about being a new recruit. The boy sniffed again. "Didn't know they was taking any more. All right, you can come over here and give me a hand while you're waiting."

Not daring to refuse, Mickey went over to the bar and began helping to unpack beer and Coke cans from the shelves under the bar. "Most of 'em prefer Coke really," said the boy. "They drink beer because they think it makes 'em look tough!" He dumped a carton of potato chips on the bar.

Mickey worked quickly, anxious to get away. He piled the last few cans on the bar and stood up. "There you are. Think I'll go and take in a bit of that car lecture. Can't start too soon."

He turned away, but the skinny boy caught his arm. "Hang on a minute, I *have* seen you before. I've been thinking about it while we were working. You were one of that lot who jumped on me in the school. And you were at the Sports Center earlier. You're one of them Irregulars."

He opened his mouth to shout, but with a fierce yank Mickey pulled him down behind the little bar. "That's right, I am—and we're working with the police!"

"You're mad. They'll kill you when I tell them."

Mickey lowered his voice to a bloodcurdling whisper. "But you're not going to tell them. If you do I'll say you're working with me and you let me in. So whatever they do to me, they'll do to you as well!"

The skinny boy stared at him.

"Listen," Mickey went on. "This place is surrounded by the Flying Squad. They're going to pounce any minute. Now, keep your mouth shut and I'll see you get off light. Come on, where's the way out?"

The skinny boy was still staring openmouthed and Mickey pulled him up and dragged him from behind the bar. "Come on," he ordered firmly. "Take me out of here. It's the only thing you can do."

Moving as if hypnotized, the other led him through a

door, along a narrow passage, and up to another door which he unlocked. "Now you close that door behind me and go back to your bar," hissed Mickey. "Soon as you get a chance you slip away—and don't say anything to anyone, or you'll be sorry!" He slipped out into the street and heard the door being closed and locked behind him. He found himself in the front entrance of the building in the blind alley Dan had first visited. He began running toward the footbridge.

Dan and the others were still on the flat roof. By now they were very anxious. Jeff had wanted to lead a rescue expedition, but Dan had vetoed it. "You saw how many there were—no point in us all getting caught. All we can do is stay here and wait. If they catch him we'll probably hear some kind of fuss. If that happens one of us will stay here on watch, and the other two go for the police." It wasn't much of a plan, but it was the best he had been able to come up with in the sudden emergency.

"I think we ought to go for the police anyway," urged Liz.

"And suppose he *hasn't* been caught," said Dan. "We could spoil his chance of getting away. If carloads of police turn up they might use him as a hostage. We'll wait."

There was a low whistle from behind them and a jubilant voice called, "Are you staying there all night, or are you coming home?"

They looked up. Mickey was waving to them from the footbridge.

# 10

## Trapped

As they made their way home through the dark streets no one was quite sure whether Mickey deserved congratulations or a clip around the ear. Indignantly Mickey pointed out that he'd *told* Dan what he was doing, and Dan had agreed! "Only because I wasn't listening to you," protested Dan.

"Then you ought to have been," said Mickey unrepentantly. Not unnaturally he was full of triumph over his adventure. "What do we do now? Go straight around to the police station?"

Dan laughed. "Can you imagine what they'd say if a gang of kids came off the streets with a story like this?"

"But that place was full of stolen stuff," said Mickey. "If that kid cracks up and tells them about me, they'll all be away in no time."

"Don't worry," said Dan reassuringly. "I'll call Day as soon as I get home. I think he'll trust me enough to go around there and take a look."

"That won't catch our Fagin, though," objected Liz. "He may not even be there tonight."

"Maybe not, but some of those kids will talk pretty quick once the police get their hands on them. That one we caught for a start—anyone dumb enough to believe Mickey's an undercover policeman. . . ."

Jeff looked at his watch. "If we don't all get home soon we'll be in trouble with more than the police—especially you, Mickey." Mickey looked at the time, gave a yell of anguish and took off like a rocket. It was already past his bedtime.

Promising to phone as soon as he had news, Dan hurried off home. To his astonishment there was a police car parked outside the door. Dan looked at it in surprise, wondering if for some reason Day had come around to see *him*. The massive figure of Day's boss, Detective Summers, emerged from the car. "Daniel Robinson?"

"Yes, of course it is," said Dan. "What can I do for you?"

"We'd like to have a word with you please—and your parents, of course."

"What about?"

Summers actually used the phrase Dan had so often read in the newspapers. "We have reason to believe you can assist us in our inquiries." A uniformed policeman and a woman police officer got out of the car and stood beside Summers.

Dan looked hard at him, and instead of using the key

rang the doorbell to fetch his mother to the door. "The police are here, Mum. They want to talk to us."

Dan's mother said apologetically, "I hope Dan hasn't been pestering you with this silly detective business? I'm afraid his father's away on business for a few days, but I promise I'll get him to speak to Dan when he gets back—ever since that business with the painting a few months ago there's been no stopping him, though of course he did get it back for you and I'm sure whatever he's done he was only trying to help . . ." Dan's mum tended to talk a lot when she was nervous.

Summers waited patiently until she ran out of breath and said, "It isn't quite like that, madam."

The seriousness in his tone quietened her down, and she moved closer to Dan. "Oh? What is it, then?"

"We've received an anonymous letter alleging that your son and his friends may be in possession of certain property. Do you mind if we take a look around?"

"Shouldn't you have a warrant?"

"Strictly speaking, we should, madam, and if you insist, my colleagues will wait here while I go and obtain one. It would be a good deal simpler if you just gave us permission now."

"Look all you want," said Dan quietly. "My room's upstairs, right at the top."

Summers looked at Dan's mother, who said, "Oh, very well, I suppose . . ." And with that the police were going through the house like a well-organized tornado. The female officer and the constable disappeared upstairs, while Summers led the way through the side passage into the garden. He stopped by the bike shed.

"There's nothing in there," said Dan's mother. "His bike was smashed up by a vandal . . ."

Summers flung open the door of the bike shed. A magnificent new bike stood leaning against the wall. "He seems to have acquired a new one pretty quick."

Dan studied the bike. It had an alloy frame, racing handlebars, tubeless tires, and every conceivable refinement, including what looked like about twenty-five Derailleur-type gears. It bore no brand name and Dan guessed it had been lovingly hand-built piece by piece, by some racing fanatic—who was probably screaming the place down at its loss.

"Do you recognize it?" asked Summers.

"I recognize it as a very expensive racing bike," said Dan. "Apart from that, I've never seen it before in my life."

Summers led the way back into the house and up the stairs to Dan's room at the top of the house.

The police constable held out a bundle of notes. "Over two hundred pound, sir. Sewn into the mattress."

"I suppose you've never seen that before either," said Summers.

Dan shook his head.

Summers turned to Dan's mother. "As I expect you know, madam, a good deal of money and property have been stolen in this neighborhood recently. We have received information that a gang of children may be involved."

"And I was the one who told you first," said Dan. "You ask Detective Constable Day."

Summers said, "I think I should warn you that we are

also visiting the homes of a number of your son's friends. I should be grateful if you could accompany your son to the station"—he used the magic phrase again—"and assist us with our inquiries."

There was pandemonium at the station. The police had visited Jeff, Liz, and Mickey. They'd found cigarettes and a hundred pounds hidden in Jeff's closet. Liz's room had yielded perfume and jewelry, and Mickey's fifty pounds and an expensive model engine. Now they were all milling around in the station foyer, bewildered children and indignant parents. Summers raised his voice. "Now I know you all want to get this distressing business over as soon as possible. So the sooner you all quiet down and let me talk to the children, the sooner you'll get home."

There was a reluctant hush. Summers said, "It would probably simplify matters if I could talk to the children alone . . ."

"Oh, no, you don't," said Dan's mother firmly. Her work often brought her into contact with courts and she knew her rights. "These children are juveniles—you are not allowed to interview them except in the presence of their parents."

"It's all right, Mum," said Dan. "We'll talk to him by ourselves."

The four Irregulars were taken into an interview room, in which was a wooden table, a cocoa-tin lid for an ashtray, and a number of rickety wooden chairs. Four chairs were arranged on one side of the table, and a single chair for Summers on the other. He sat down and arranged a pile of papers in front of him. A police stenographer with notebook and pencil sat at a smaller table in the corner. Suddenly the whole atmosphere became very much like a courtroom. A uniformed policeman stood by the door, and a moment later Detective Constable Day slipped into the room and stood beside him. He winked at Dan over Summers' shoulder, but his thin face was pale and tense. For the first time Dan began to realize that things were really serious.

When Summers spoke, his voice was unexpectedly kindly. "Now, I don't know what you have been up to, but we've got you bang to rights. I daresay it all started off as a bit of a lark, eh? Dabbling in crime for kicks. Then you got mixed up with professionals and it all got out of hand." He paused. "Now then, the best thing for everybody is if you tell me all about it. You're all kids from good homes, you're classed as juveniles anyway, so we can't send you to prison or even reform school, come to that—chances are you'll get off with a lecture from the bench and a suspended sentence. Now why don't you just tell me all about it, and we can all go home?"

Seeing the usually stern-faced Summers in the role of kindly old uncle was too much for Dan. Despite the seriousness of the situation he nearly burst out laughing. "I'm sorry, Sergeant, but it won't work."

Immediately Summers' face returned to its usual hard and threatening expression. "What won't, sonny?"

"The soft approach. We haven't got anything to tell you. None of us have seen any of that money before, or the other things. It was all planted on us."

"Oh, yes? Who by?"

"The people we've been after—the people you're after too, if you only knew it." He turned to the police stenographer. "I should like to make a statement, please. You'd better send the others out, and take statements from them separately, then you can compare."

Summers gave Dan a baffled look, feeling that somehow things were being taken out of his hands. "All right, I'm in charge here, if you don't mind."

He turned to the constable. "Take these three outside, we'll get their statements later." Liz, Jeff, and Mickey went out, and there was a babble of voices from outside as they tried to reassure their parents.

Dan drew a deep breath, marshaling his thoughts. Then, in a firm, calm voice, he dictated a complete account of his involvement with the case, starting with his interest in the robberies and covering the trap in the school, the attack on Baskerville, and the smashing of his bike, the visits to the youth clubs, the attack in the parking lot and finally their visit to the club that was supposed to be shut. "I was on my way to see you about that tonight," concluded Dan. "If I were you, I'd get someone around there right away."

"Better just check it out, eh, Sarge?" said Day hurriedly, and disappeared from the room before Summers could stop him.

The night seemed to go on and on. First Summers took Dan through his statement point by point, trying to shake him on every little detail. Then statements were taken from the others, and they were questioned about them. They were all questioned again separately, and all questioned again together. They were cajoled and persuaded and given cups of tea and sandwiches, they were bullied and hectored and threatened with the full majesty of the law.

Sometime during all this Day reappeared and reported on his visit to the abandoned youth club under the railway arch. "Empty, Sarge. Nothing and nobody."

"Was it now?" said Summers and gave Dan a triumphant glare.

"But someone had been using it," said Day hurriedly. "There were signs a lot of stuff had been moved out and one of our patrol cars reported a trailer truck in the area."

Summers gave a baffled growl, and went on with his questions.

Much, much later, when they were all being questioned in the interview room again, Dan stood up. In a voice hoarse from talking he said, "I've had enough of this. We've all told our stories about fifty times each, and we won't change them one little bit because they happen to be the truth. This whole thing is an obvious frame-up." He looked at the hard-faced police officer. "We all helped you solve a big case not long ago; why should we suddenly start stealing things?"

Summers muttered something about "doing it for kicks."

"I get my kicks from solving crimes, not committing them. And if I did turn crooked, I should hope I'm a lot brighter than this." He paused for breath. "Look at that bike—an expensive hand-built racing model, easily identifiable, just stuck in my shed. Bundles of money under the pillow. Liz has got no time for perfume or jewelry anyway, and Jeff is too much of an athletics nut even to think of smoking."

"What about the money?" demanded Summers. "Are you telling me someone would chuck that away just to frame you all?"

"Three hundred and fifty quid," jeered Dan. "How many thousands have been stolen in all these robberies?"

Summers didn't answer. Dan slumped back in his chair. "Anyway, you can please yourself. Charge us or let us go. I'm not saying another word."

"And nor will we," said Liz. Jeff and Mickey nodded.

Summers looked around at their determined faces. Gathering his papers, he stood up. "Put 'em back with their parents. I'm going to see the station inspector."

Dan and the others were taken to the larger interview room and reunited with their parents. Dan gave his mother a hug. "Cheer up, Mum, not much longer."

But it was quite a while longer before Summers came back into the room. In a wooden voice he said, "It has been decided that for the moment no charges will be made, as we wish to pursue further inquiries. I must ask you to bring the children involved back to the station at eleven A.M. the day after tomorrow. You will then be informed as to whether further proceedings will be taken."

Wearily, children and parents said subdued goodnights and straggled out of the station. One by one the Irregulars got into their parents' cars and were driven home. As Dan was about to get in his mother's car, Day appeared on the steps. "Doesn't look too good," he said in a hurried whisper. "Summers wanted to charge you all with criminal conspiracy, bring you up in the magistrate's court. Inspector Rogers is still a bit dubious, reckons there's something fishy going on. Doesn't want to get sued for wrongful arrest! But unless we turn up something quick, I reckon Summers will persuade him there's no alternative. In that case you'll all be charged day after tomorrow."

Dan yawned. "Thanks, Happy. I'm too tired to worry about it now, though." He got into the car and it drove away.

When Mickey got home his dad had come home from the pub to find his wife and son missing and was noisily demanding to know what was going on. Mickey's mum poured out the story amid floods of tears.

Mickey's dad put an enormous hand on his small son's shoulder. "You haven't been nicking stuff, have you, son?" he said threateningly. Mickey glared indignantly back at him. "No, I haven't. It was a frame-up."

His father stared searchingly at him. Then, "Of course it was, son," he said gently. "Don't worry, it'll all be sorted out. Any chance of a bit of bread and cheese, Mother? Dare say Mickey's hungry too."

Grumbling through her tears, Mickey's mum went to the bread bin.

Liz's mum was in a state of high excitement, her journalist's instincts going full blast. "We'll make a national scandal of it. Police brutality, kids dragged out of their beds and questioned all night. I'll contact some of the action groups. There are several MP's who might be interested . . ."

In a choked voice Liz said, "Look, Mum, this isn't one of your crusades. It isn't women's lib or prisoner's rights, it's *me*!" Liz's mum stared at her daughter and hugged her consolingly.

"Sorry, love, you know us journalists. Sell our own mother for a story . . ."

Jeff's parents were probably the hardest hit. They were quiet, conventional people—his father was assistant manager at a local bank—and never in their whole lives had they had the slightest brush with the law. As far as they were concerned, the presence of a police car outside the door meant social disgrace. And surely Jeff must be guilty of something, or why would the police have come?

As Jeff went up to bed, his father said awkwardly, "You know your mum and I will stand by you, whatever happens . . ."

"Thanks a lot," said Jeff bitterly. "It'd be even nicer if you'd believe I hadn't done anything." He went up to bed.

Dan's mother was pottering about the kitchen, getting them a late-night snack. "Of course the treatment of juvenile offenders has always been a social problem," she was saying. "Really, the provisions are quite inadequate."

Dan grinned affectionately at her. If they sent him to prison she'd lecture him on the deficiencies in the penal system on visiting day. He finished his cocoa, gave her a kiss, and went on up to his room. But he didn't go to bed. Instead he got out the Fagin File, curled up in his old armchair, and began reading through it. Not until far into the night did he put the file away and go to bed. He was pretty sure he knew who Fagin was . . . but now he himself was discredited and accused. Who was going to believe him?

# 11

---

# Outlawed

When Dan arrived in the school playground next morning, an excited crowd gathered around him. "How did you get out, Robbo?" someone shouted. "Have you broken jail?" "What about a share of the loot?" yelled someone else. Across the playground Liz and Jeff were getting the same treatment, and when Mickey turned up, everyone jumped on him, calling him Al Capone and demanding to know if he'd robbed any good banks lately.

At the beginning of school, they were collared by an anxious monitor and told the Headmaster wanted to see them, right away. The interview was brief. Old Fusspot said although he personally was quite sure the whole thing was a ghastly mistake, perhaps it would be better if they stayed away from school for a day or two. "Particularly in view of the rather unhealthy interest in your predicament shown by your fellow pupils . . ."

Liz started to protest, but Dan shushed her. "I'm sure you're right, sir," he said soothingly. "Much the best thing. I would like to talk to you alone for a few minutes . . ." Anxious to be rid of them, the Headmaster agreed, and Jeff, Liz, and Mickey went outside to wait for Dan.

He joined them a few minutes later, and as they walked across the playground, Jeff felt every window in the school concealed a crowd of curious faces. "I feel like Capone leaving Alcatraz," he muttered. Mickey, who was rather enjoying his role of dangerous criminal, turned around and shot out all the school windows with an imaginary machine gun.

Liz turned to Dan. "What's going to happen?" she asked anxiously. "I'm finding all this a bit of a strain."

"Do you think they'll charge us?" asked Jeff. "Will we have to appear in court?" He was thinking about his parents.

"We might," admitted Dan. "Unless we do something about it ourselves."

"But what can we do?"

"Catch Fagin."

"Just like that?" asked Liz incredulously. "We don't even know who he is."

"I've had an idea for some time," said Dan. He told them of his interview with the Headmaster. "All we've got to do now is prove it. We've got just one day, so we mustn't waste time. I worked it all out last night. There's a job for everybody."

The headquarters of Anglo-Consolidated was a black-glass skyscraper that towered above the older city buildings like some gloomy giant. The Chairman's office on the fourteenth floor was sacred. When a thin, fair girl in jeans and sweater walked straight past the receptionist and into the holy of holies, the receptionist was too astonished at first to protest.

She ran after the girl to bring her back, but by that time the intruder was already talking to the Chairman. "I haven't got time to go through your sixteen secretaries," said Liz. "I've got to talk to you now about something urgent. Innocent people are in trouble, and you've got to help us."

The burly silver-haired man behind the enormous desk put down his huge cigar. "I admire push," he said in an unexpectedly mild voice. "It's push that got me where I am." He waved the receptionist away and looked at Liz. "You've got three minutes."

It was considerably more than three minutes later when the Chairman buzzed his secretary. "Take down this letter, type it immediately, bring it back for signature, and give it to this young lady." He started to dictate.

When Jeff's father came out of the bank at lunch time, he was in a state of harassed preoccupation. Everyone at the bank had been very kind, but it was obvious they'd all heard what had happened. Somehow he couldn't help feeling his chances of promotion to manager were receding fast. He heard a familiar voice. "Hello, Dad."

It was Jeff. For a moment he felt an irrational impulse to avoid his own son, then, ashamed, he said, "Jeff! What are you doing here? Has something happened?"

Jeff shook his head. "I need your help, that's all."

"I'll do anything I can, you know that."

Jeff said wryly, "The trouble is, Dad, I want you to do something a bit illegal."

For one awful moment Jeff's father wondered if his criminal son was enlisting his cooperation in a bank robbery.

Then he saw Jeff's anxious face and said stoutly, "Never you mind that, son. If it'll help you out of trouble—I'll do it!"


The head salesman in the big West End car showroom studied his reflection in the big plate-glass window and straightened his tie. He brushed nonexistent dust from the shoulder of his immaculate suit and surveyed his kingdom of cars. All the most expensive models on the market lined up in gleaming array. Rolls, Jaguars, Bentleys, and of course the more expensive foreign makes.

Suddenly he became aware of a jarring element. A small boy, an urchin, had actually wandered into the showroom. He wore scruffy jeans and denim jacket and sneakers, he had enormous ears and a cheeky grin.

The head salesman looked down on him from his superior height. "May I help you?" he inquired frostily.

Mickey grinned. "Yes. I've come to have a chat about buying a sports car. . . ."

Dan Robinson looked crushed by misfortune as he slunk down into the foyer of the Sports Center. He was looking around guiltily, as if he expected a policeman's hand to fall on his shoulder.

Chris Vosper hurried out of the office as soon as he saw him. "Dan, I heard about the trouble. If there's anything I can do . . ."

"As a matter of fact, there is," said Dan gratefully.

"Then you name it, old son. If you need money for a lawyer or anything like that . . ."

"No, it's not that. The thing is, we've all got to be at the police station at ten tomorrow for a sort of inquiry. They're going to decide if they'll charge us or not. Would you be willing to come and be a sort of witness for me?"

Chris hesitated. "Well, I'd like to help, Dan, you know that. But I've already given a statement to the police about the parking lot business."

"Please," said Dan. "You could be a sort of character witness as well. If someone like you spoke up for me, they'd be more likely to listen."

Chris Vosper slapped him on the back. "All right, Dan. I don't know if it'll do you any good, but I'll be there."

Dan cheered up. "Thanks, Chris. You don't know how much better that makes me feel. . . ."

Detective Constable Day finished his tea and lowered his voice so that the words were almost drowned by the

clatter of the market café. "It's asking a lot, Dan."

"I know it is—but it's my only chance. Even if these charges don't stick, they'll leave a nasty smear behind. This is the only way we can prove we're innocent. It's only a few bank inquiries—you've already got the information from Jeff's dad to go on. Oh, and don't forget the fingerprints . . ."

"All right. There's not much time, but I'll do what I can."

Dan got up to leave. "Thanks. See you at ten tomorrow then." He handed over a bulging file. "Here, you'd better show him this, first thing in the morning."

Detective Sergeant Summers closed the Fagin File and handed it back to Day, who was waiting anxiously. He said nothing.

"You've got to admit it all holds together, Sarge," said Day persuasively.

Summers nodded almost reluctantly. "You're really sticking your neck out for these kids, aren't you, Happy?"

"Why not?" said Day cheerfully. "Come on, Sarge, you know it was a frame-up. Someone's making idiots of us. Wouldn't it be nice to get the right bloke?"

Summers sighed. "All right, Happy, you can give it a go. But watch your step, you're not dealing with a nobody. You say the kids are already here?"

"All in the interview room. They turned up an hour early to try to get it over before their parents came."

"What about their character witness?"

"He'll be along any minute." The roar of a powerful

engine came from the street and Day grinned. "In fact, I think he's here now!"

When Chris Vosper came into the big interview room, Dan and the rest of the Irregulars were sitting upright on their chairs, looking just like prisoners in the dock. A very large policeman stood by the door, and an even larger one in plain clothes stood beside him.

Detective Constable Day was in the seat on the other side of the table, and he jumped up as Chris came in. "Very good of you to come and assist us with our inquiries, sir. Have a seat."

A chair was brought for Chris and placed on the other side of the table from Day, who leaned forward, shuffling through some papers in a file.

"Now then, sir," he began cheerfully. "You are Mr. Christopher Vosper of Ducane Mansions?" He paused and said chattily, "That's that new penthouse block on the top of the hill, isn't it? Nice flats, those. Must cost a few bob to rent. About fifty pounds a week, I reckon?"

"Something like that," said Chris, amused.

Day plowed on. "And the very handsome Lamborghini that's making our police cars look shabby—yours as well?"

"That's right," said Chris curtly. "What's all this about? I understand I was here to be some kind of character witness for Dan."

"All in good time, sir. Must establish the character of the character witness. Now then, you are employed as part-time assistant at the Sports Center at a nominal salary of twenty pounds a week?" Day gave Chris a look of innocent curiosity. "May I ask how you manage to enjoy such a handsome standard of living on that rather limited income?"

Chris shrugged impatiently. "It's scarcely any secret that my father's a millionaire. Shortage of money has never been one of my problems. Now then . . ."

Suddenly Day changed the subject. "Why did you leave school so suddenly? Promising career, university scholarship . . ."

"I just got bored with it all. I was telling Dan about it."

Dan reached across and took the file from Day. "I've got a note from the Headmaster here, Chris. He says you were expelled—for breaking into his study to get a look at the 'A' level papers. Your father was a big school benefactor. He persuaded poor Old Fusspot to keep it quiet."

Chris was beginning to look trapped now. "Look, that's all in the past . . ."

"Nice of your dad to look after you so well," said Jeff. "Eight thousand pounds in your current account."

"I thought a man's bank account was confidential—"

Jeff grinned. "I just happen to have a useful contact."

Day looked at a slip of paper. "Not to mention another seven thousand in an account under the name of Vickery. Your pocket money must be really something!"

"You paid cash for that Lamborghini too," said Mickey. "I found the Sale Room. Remembered you very well, they did."

"My father gives me whatever I ask for," said Chris

defiantly. "Money means nothing to him, he's got more than you can imagine . . ."

It was Liz's turn to take the file. "I've a letter here from your father, Chris, dated yesterday." She read aloud. "I have given my son Christopher no financial support for some years, nor do I intend to do so. After he was expelled from school I gave him opportunities in a number of our branches around the world—in each one he managed to incur heavy debts, which he tried to pay off by defrauding the firm. I finally dismissed him in Australia with enough money for his ticket home. Since his return to England I have had no more communication with him. I write this letter with the greatest reluctance, only because I am assured that he has now involved innocent children in his schemes."

"You can't prove anything," muttered Chris. "All right, so I've got money. I've always had money . . ."

Day leaned forward to deliver the final crushing blow. "You were up on a fraud charge in Aussie last year. Your dad got it squashed, but you were fingerprinted. We've just got a copy of the prints through. They match with a thumb print on the boiler of that model engine we found in Mickey's room."

Chris seemed to crumple before their eyes, the handsome sophisticated figure cringing like a child. "You can't prove it was me . . . I want a lawyer . . ."

Detective Sergeant Summers came forward, with a kind of savage eagerness. "Whatever for, sir? You haven't been charged with anything. You're just helping us with our inquiries . . ."

Before Summers could start his interrogation, Dan said, "What about us, Sergeant?"

Summers looked at the Irregulars as if he'd never seen them before. "Hoppit," he said briefly. Thankfully they hurried out. Dan paused at the door, and saw that Summers had drawn his chair close to Chris. "Now then, Chris," he was saying in a friendly voice, "what about all this loose money in your bank account, eh?"

Chris gave the detective a look that was wary and scared and defiant all at the same time. Suddenly Dan realized. Chris had acquired The Look. And Summers had recognized it. He would pursue his victim now until he brought him down. Feeling as if he were leaving an inexperienced fox with a large and savage foxhound, Dan followed the others from the room.

Day came with them. "Your troubles are over," he announced jubilantly.

"You think he'll talk?" asked Dan.

"Talk?" said Day. "He'll sing like a bird. I know the type. He'll hold out for about half an hour and then it'll all come pouring out."

He saw them on to the police station steps, where puzzled parents were just arriving, demanding to know why their children had sneaked off to the station early. Day held up his hand. "Nothing to worry about, ladies and gents. You can take it from me, all charges will be dropped. Your kids have been completely exonerated! In fact, you might say it's another brilliant triumph for the Baker Street Irregulars. Now if you'll excuse me, I've got to go and talk to a man about a bank account!"

# 12

# The Last Attack

When Dan called at the police station next day, he learned that everything had happened as Day predicted. Chris confessed everything, his penniless return to England, his scheme for involving children in crime, the way he'd made contact with Sikes, whose real name was Simpson, and recruited his team from the tough kids in and around the Estate. The next step had been to make contact with a group of professional criminals, who had agreed to use the old youth club as a storehouse of stolen goods, and a sort of training school. The rash of local burglaries had been a kind of pilot scheme. With professional backing Chris had planned to expand into other areas of London, and to go into pickpocketing and car theft as well.

The burly motorcycle thug Simpson—or Sikes, as

he'd called himself—seemed to have got clear away, but thanks to Chris's detailed confession, most of the kids in the gang had been caught, including the wiry little Rattray—who was still protesting he didn't know anything about anything.

"What'll happen to them all?" asked Dan.

"Not a lot," said Day. "They're all juveniles, there's not much you *can* do to them. Can't send them to prison, can't even send 'em to reform school. Most they'll get is a lecture from the judge, maybe a few fines. That was the beauty of Chris's scheme. His labor force was so young they weren't really risking much, even though they were involved in quite serious crimes. Chris himself is a different matter, though. I reckon he'll be in for it."

"Well, it was all his idea," said Dan. "Can't help feeling sorry for him, though."

"What first put you on to him?"

"He told Mickey he drove his car back from Rome— yet according to his own story, he came home as a penniless hippie. So if he was willing to tell a trivial lie just to impress Mickey . . ."

"Was that all?"

"He was always a bit off key, somehow. Too glamorous for a do-gooder. At first I thought he was too rich to be involved. Then I suddenly thought, who needs money so much as someone who's always been well off and is suddenly without it? I started to wonder if his father really was such a forgiving type. . . ."

"He was only an amateur really," said Day scornfully. "Once we started checking up on him, everything just collapsed. He was like one of those buildings in a Western—all false front!"

"Poor old Chris," said Dan sadly. "I wonder what went wrong?"

"You get 'em like that sometimes—your charming psychopath. No sense of right or wrong, just doesn't mean anything to them."

"I suppose it all started at school," said Dan thoughtfully. "He knew he'd never get enough 'A' levels to take up that place at Oxford, so he tried to cheat. Even though that didn't work, he just went on cheating. He'd always had plenty of cash, so he thought it was a kind of right." Dan sighed, then cheered up. "Well, I must be off. Baskerville's coming home from the vet today."

"Soppy great thing," said Day. "Lot of use he was, wasn't he? I'd get yourself a nice fierce Pekinese if I were you."

As he led a jubilant Baskerville home from the vet, Dan reluctantly felt that Day was right. Baskerville had been trained as a guard dog sometime in the past, but his basic amiability had made him unsuitable for the work. Dan ruffled the great dog's head. "Don't know what fierce is, do you?" he teased.

Baskerville gave a contented *woof* as their house came in sight. He seemed quite his old self again, though the bald patch on his head gave him a faintly comical appearance, like a canine monk.

Dan let them in and Baskerville bounded hopefully to his feeding bowl. Obviously they hadn't kept his favorite brand of dog meat at the hospital.

Dan tipped a whole can of meat into the bowl, filled the water dish, and wandered upstairs. His mother was still at work, so he was alone in the house. He decided to use the peace and quiet to bring the Fagin File up to date. But when he looked on his desk, the file wasn't there. Puzzled, Dan looked around the room. Had he put it into his closet? He sometimes used the top shelf for storing things. He opened the closet door, and a giant black-clad figure sprang out at him like some demon jack-in-the-box. It was Sikes.

With a sweep of his arm, Sikes sent Dan staggering onto the bed. The Fagin File was clutched in his left hand; there was a steel bar in his right. He stepped around the bed, barring Dan's way to the door. "I've been having a nice little read," he announced. "Think you're clever, don't you? Well, now you're going to pay for it. Thanks to you a nice little racket's broken up, Chris is singing his head off, and I'm on the run. But before I disappear, I'm going to do for you . . ."

He raised the steel bar—and Baskerville padded into the room, looking for Dan. At the sight of Sikes, he tensed, and growled deep in his throat.

Sikes laughed, "You needn't think he'll save you. I settled him before when I smashed your bike. He'll just get another dose of the same."

Dan's first thought was that Baskerville mustn't be hurt again. "Go!" he ordered. "Downstairs."

Baskerville ignored him. Stiff-legged he stalked toward Sikes. The steel bar flashed high—and Baskerville sprang. He caught the arm with the bar and pulled Sikes to the ground, dragging him to and fro with a dreadful growling sound. Sikes began to scream. As he scrambled from the bed, Dan realized what had happened. The savage blow on the head had taught Baskerville one vital lesson—not everyone in the world was his friend.

Dan shouted down at the writhing Sikes, "Keep still! Shut up and keep still and I'll try to call him off."

Sikes collapsed sobbing and Dan snapped, "Baskerville! Let go!"

With obvious reluctance the dog obeyed. Sikes got to his feet clutching his bleeding wrist, and again the dog gave that low, terrible growl. Sikes froze.

"Guard, Baskerville," said Dan, hoping it was the right command. He looked at Sikes. "We're going to walk downstairs now. There's a phone in the kitchen— I'm going to dial nine-nine-nine."

Sikes glared at him, looking around like a trapped animal.

"You're welcome to make a run for it if you like," said Dan steadily. "Only—I can't guarantee to get him off you a second time."

Dan picked up the iron bar in a handkerchief, so as not to spoil the fingerprints, tossed the Fagin File back on his desk, and led the way down to the kitchen.

Baskerville stayed very close to Sikes all the way, letting out the occasional rumbling growl. He sat beside him, staring unwinkingly while Dan dialed the police. When the police car skidded around the corner, Dan led the way to the front step, and Sikes walked very slowly beside him.

Dan handed over burglar and steel bar and promised to call in the station later to make a statement.

To the accompaniment of a final growl from Baskerville, Sikes got into the police car. Dan had the distinct impression that he was glad to go. . . .

# Epilogue

It ended, as it had begun, with a group photograph. Not outside the nonexistent 221B Baker Street, but outside the local police station. It had been Liz's mother's idea. She'd turned up at the police station with four grinning Irregulars, Baskerville, and the same trendy photographer who'd once tried to persuade Dan to put on a deerstalker.

"The thing is, Sergeant Summers," she said firmly, "it would be a nice gesture, wouldn't it? I mean, we all know the police were acting under a misapprehension, but the mud from this sort of accusation tends to stick. Now an official statement from you saying how much

Dan and his friends have helped, accompanied by a suitable photograph, could put all that right."

Summers frowned. "Grateful as we are for the assistance of the public, it is not the policy of the police . . ." he began.

Liz's mother interrupted him. "I mean that would be *so* much nicer than an article about the incompetence of policemen who have to let a gang of kids solve their crimes for them."

Summers was outraged. "That's no better than blackmail," he sputtered. "In a police station, too!"

"Call it good public relations, Sarge," suggested Day, and eventually Summers agreed.

They showed Dan's father the photograph when he got back home a few days later. It was on the front page of the local paper, and it showed Detective Sergeant Summers standing on the police station steps between Dan and Jeff, his arm around their shoulders in a fatherly embrace. His heavy features were twisted into what looked like a grimace of pain, but was presumably intended to be a benign smile.

In front of this unlikely trio stood Liz and Mickey, with Baskerville in the middle. The headline above the picture read:   TOP COP CONGRATULATES CLEARED CRIME BUSTERS. Dan's father winced and put the paper down. "Well, I prefer the picture to the prose."

Dan looked at the picture again. "It's quite good, isn't it. He's not bad, that photographer—Liz's mum brought him along again. He took that other one of us all in Baker Street." Dan smiled reminiscently. "He was quite surprised when I told him lots of people think Sherlock Holmes is still alive and well."

Dan's father looked at him thoughtfully. "Do they? Well, I'm not so sure they're wrong!"